PAUL ST. PIERRE

Tell me a good lie

TALES FROM THE CHILCOTIN COUNTRY

D0168396

Douglas & McIntyre

VANCOUVER/TORONTO

Dedicated to the old timers, sons of bitches included.

Douglas & McIntyre Ltd.
2323 Quebec Street, Suite 201
Vancouver, British Columbia V5T 4S7

CANADIAN CATALOGUING IN PUBLICATION DATA
St. Pierre, Paul, 1923–
    Tell me a good lie.

    ISBN 1-55054-863-8

    I. Title.
PS8537.A54T44 2001   C813'.54   C2001-910009-4
PR9199.3.S16T44 2001

Some of the pieces in this book were previously published in *Chilcotin
Holiday* and *Chilcotin and Beyond*. Others are collected here in book
form for the first time.

Editing by Brian Scrivener
Typeset by Tanya Lloyd/Spotlight Designs
Cover design by Jim Skipp
Cover photograph by Vance Hanna
Printed and bound in Canada by Friesens
Printed on acid-free paper ∞

We gratefully acknowledge the financial support of the Canada Council
for the Arts, the British Columbia Ministry of Tourism, Small Business and
Culture, and the Government of Canada through the Book Publishing
Industry Development Program (BPIDP) for our publishing activities.

Contents

Prologue 1

Everything You Need to Make a Ranch 9

Lessons from a Swimming Eagle 12

Seeing the Neighbour's Light 15

Seeking the Sound of Silence 18

Alas, a Land Not Fit for Camp Robbers 21

Poplars Rustle, Pines Sigh 24

Chilcotin Wears Laceup Shoes 27

The Ritual Drunkups 30

Ode to Godawful Roads 33

Bad Roads Built Character 36

Getting Lost is Half the Fun 39

Trees of Ivory and Gold 42

The Lady Hunts Sheep 45

How a Hello Girl Goes Hiking 48

Mickey's Cougar 51

The Education of Fly 54

Namko's Coolee Chilco 58

A Place Lost and Lovely 61

The View from the Wineglass 64

How Red Lost His Ranch 67

iii

Joe's Electric and the Truck That Drove Itself 70
Perce's Rubber Worm 73
Kitchen Midden 76
The Cariboo Alligator 80
A Judicial View of the Cariboo Alligator 85
The Sidehill Gouger Situation 88
The Land Where Diogenes Put Out His Lantern 91
The Corporate Beef Drive 94
Longhorns, Again, at the Oldest Ranch 98
The Man Who Built the Sky Ranch 101
Ollie Nickolaye, Who Was Loved 105
The Father of the Groom 108
The Man with the Extra Airport 111
Looking for Horses 114
Looking for Horses Again 117
Mustangs and Other Horses 120
On Old Horses, Winter, and Death 124
The Wild Horse Hunter 127
Horse Doctoring 130
Horses, Horses, Horses 133
Chilcotin's Last Great Horse 136
Country People Don't Count 139
Line Up, Pay Up, Shut Up 142
You Want a Bridge? Then Build a Bridge 145
Stealthy, Healthy and Wise 148
Incident at Duke Martin Bridge 151
A Non-Romance in the Moose Country 154
Spring Breakup 157
Silent Ken 160
How to Die Chilcotin Style 164
The Old House on Twinflowers 167
Ruined by Clean Living 170

Prologue

These are 52 tales, new and old, about the Chilcotin Country. They are gathered here amid the lengthening shadows of a late afternoon. If some seem strange, remember that they come from the land where Diogenes finally doused the lantern. If some of those from a half-century ago seem warmer than those written in this age of Big Brother, Newspeak, Wrongthink and the other Orwellian horrors, forgive me. I am like an old man lusting after young women.

To know the old Chilcotin Country is gone and is not going to come back, drive the old stage road between Williams Lake and Anahim Lake on blacktop, the car on cruise control and two local radio stations coming in loud and clear.

You meet a truck delivering bottled water. Yuppywater in Chilcotin, land of the wild and free rivers? He's making a profit selling it, you can bet, otherwise he wouldn't be here. Over another rise, confident his radar detector won't squeal, comes a sporty Pontiac, driven by a civil servant who commutes between Williams Lake and Alexis Creek. Commuting, to Alexis. Well, well.

Wasn't it only the day before yesterday that the woman guest complained at the log cabin Chilcotin Hotel that she had no night light when the power plant shut down at midnight? Sammy

Barrowman, the owner, who boasted his hotel had the only flush toilets between Williams Lake and Yokohama, was severe with her: "Madam, have you any conception of how far it is to the next hotel?" Not far now, Sammy—commuting distance.

In the days of the old dirt road, there weren't many vehicles of any kind. Red McCue's big delivery truck ("Get the Hill Out of My Way" read its motto) was called The Stage, for reasons unknown. There never was a stagecoach on the plateau. When the occasional government inspector turned up with weigh scales it was the duty of any traveller to warn Red to dump his overload into the jack pines until he'd been weighed.

At the start of Cariboo Flats, where the last migrating caribou band was shot out to zero in the 1940s, was an emergency cabin for travellers. When you came over this road in winter at 40 below—the temperature which used to come here and stay—a wise driver checked his mileage gauge from one house lantern light to the next. You needed to know, if your vehicle quit, which was the shortest walk to safety because you could not walk far at 40 below. Emergency cabins served where the road ran too long between lantern lights.

Ike Singh, the Chinese Canadian with the East Indian name, often used those cabins when trucking in to his general store in Anahim Lake. He'd bought the store from Stan Dowling who, in the 1930s, brought the first gas-powered vehicle into Anahim, driving on wagon roads, cattle trails and frozen lakes, because no complete road yet existed.

Lester Dorsey was then still running pack trains over Precipice to tidewater for the Hudson's Bay Company. Like more than one man, he'd come up here on the run. He was making his horse rear at a country fair in Washington State when the horse came down on a citizen's head. Lester ran until he couldn't run any farther. Years later, someone from his home town found him and told him, laughing, "The son of a bitch got up and walked away, Lester."

Now, policemen with radar on the road? There used to be only one—count, one—policeman for the whole area, which is about a third the size of France.

At least half of the highway's shiny pickup trucks are driven by First Nations people. Week before last—wasn't it?—they rode saddle horse or moved in wagons drawn by half-broke cayuses. It took them days, not a few hours, to get to the Williams Lake Stampede from the western side of the plateau, and days to get home again. Those who got drunk (and everybody worthwhile was supposed to get drunk at Stampede time) were thrown in jail. Public drunkenness was then a criminal offence. The ranchers for whom they cowboyed would phone the police to locate their strays and request that they be turned loose on the promise that the rancher would be in town to post bail for them some time real soon.

Today the Indians have big cab pickups, hydro, TV, Internet connections, handsome band administration offices and lots of city lawyers on their payroll, some of whom are themselves natives. Finally, they have a heaping great pile of grievances and land claims. Instead of the occasional drunk-up at Stampede and other occasions, there is now continuous heavy drinking which peaks on the day the welfare cheques arrive. The suicide rate is well above the national average.

In the old days—must we note one more time that they aren't really that old?—many of these people had the reputation, "Good man in the bush, poor man in town." Although some might like to deny it now, the whites tended to treat them as second-class citizens, and a few would say no *Siwash* matured beyond the age of 14. However, there were also deep and lifelong friendships across the racial lines, and a lot of mutual respect.

This raises the question of whether today's First Nations people, provided with schools, health services and limitless forms of counselling and aid, are happier than in the years when they got by, proudly but thinly, by cowboying, shooting squirrels and taking hay contracts. It takes a wiser man than I to answer that question. However, the same question can be raised about whites. Throughout this nation, cities, towns and villages are far better places to live than they were half a century ago. I know of no exceptions to that rule. But how many communities are happier places today? Are any? I am persuaded that the happiness of societies does rise and fall, but it does not do so in synchronization with the society's material prosperity. Man is an economic animal to only a limited extent, and dollars can never satisfy the hungers of his soul.

Whatever the case, the evidence of material prosperity is everywhere in this country, which was once the last stand of the North American open-range cattle rancher, driven here out of the settled places to the high, cold land at the northwestern edge of the continent's grasslands, still searching for the independence he never found. Logging long ago replaced ranching as the cash cow. It is the driving force of the economy in a region which never expected to see payrolls, regular work hours, paid holidays, sick time and unions.

The chattering classes hate the loggers, ostensibly because of clearcutting, in truth because they are guilty of making money. As for the clearcutting, that was always nature's way here in the Lodgepole Pine forests, but in the old days it was fire, not tree snippers, that bared the ground. Those fires, sometimes, were set by ranchers intent on opening up new land to grass and cattle. The ranchers hadn't much use for loggers either, but in their case it was for the usual reason—that they had failed to become ranchers.

The land is now in comfortable middle age, fatter, slower, even a bit stodgy. Certainly much less rich in God's great gift of foolishness. Now it has the Internet, 200-channel TV satellite dishes, and marijuana grow operations, both the outdoor and the indoor kind. Although no community is big enough to have a resident lawyer, two lawyers might make a living in one or two places.

Of course, as elsewhere, once a place has blacktop, stop signs, plumbing inspectors and grief counsellors, lovers of the wilderness are never far behind. They come with their placards, their strange slogans and their irritating habit of telling the locals that they know not the harm they do the environment or the wickedness that is theirs. They can claim as much right to be here as anyone. There is nothing wrong with mortgage payers, pro- and anti-abortionists or people who like McDonald's hamburgers. They have as much right to be here as the people before them, although one might wish they hadn't lost the priceless gift of being able to laugh at themselves.

A few traces of the past are to be found. Many a ranch house, well supplied with reliable BC Hydro, keeps a wood cook stove because the woman of the house insists on it. However, no woman has yet been sighted who wants to return to the days before refrigeration, drying moosemeat—"the Queen's beef"—in the sun to make jerky. Men who meet after a few months apart still ask the one important question: "How'd ya winter?" How you wintered was once a life-and-death affair. Also a regular form of greeting is "Tell me a good lie." You will hear a gas siphon called a Chilcotin credit card, and people will say that when a Chilcotin woman has twins there are four of them. Old Chinook words still spot conversations, *hiyu, hiyas, skookum, mesachie, cultus* (many, big, strong, wicked, useless). But all that is fading, fading, fading fast in this land which once occupied a position just on the outer edge of probability.

Those now called old timers must have been among the world's most self-reliant people. Nothing seemed impossible once they made up their minds to do it. Norman Lee drove cattle to the Klondike gold rush, and Dick Church drove a tractor the full length of Big Creek one winter to pull out a wrecked plane.

Neither Norman nor Dick made a nickel on their projects, yet neither regretted trying. Those people asked nothing of the government and were neither surprised nor disappointed when nothing was exactly what they got.

The situation is different now. Government is viewed less as an unwelcome nuisance and more as a powerful and malevolent opponent. When Wayne Plummer's hay meadow cabin burned to the ground while left alone and untended, the police were curious. "Mr. Plummer, does anyone hold a grudge against you? Can you think of anybody who wants to do you harm?" He thought a while and said, "Only the government."

One must beware. Few things are more tiresome than old farts going on and on about the good old days. The old days weren't all good in Chilcotin. The land had its share of faults. There weren't many murders, but there also weren't many people either, and statisticians might find the murder rate was high. The justice rate was low. One of two commissioners appointed to investigate a death, there being no coroner, reported, "He was beat up pretty bad, but we figured if his heart hadn't stopped he'd still be alive, so we put it down as heart trouble."

Too many young men knew no other form of social life than getting falling-down drunk before the Saturday night dance was two hours old. Teachers in one-room log cabins, still less ranch wives, teaching their own kids in kitchen classes, could do little to bring the great, exciting outside world into the lives of the young. It was a country okay for Swedes and grizzly bears, but hard on horses and schoolteachers.

I am reminded of one ranch wife who said, "I'm almost sixty and there are only three things I can do well. I can handle a wood stove, I make good bread, and I can back up a five-horse trailer." Or another, Mickey Dorsey, heroic wife of the heroic Lester, who noted that in ranch life the day always came when a mother could no longer tell her daughters from her sons. They could rope and ride and doctor sick horses. "They'll make wonderful wives for ranchers, but that is all they will ever know."

Why were they in Chilcotin, this happy little band of people, individualistic, resourceful, independent and, buried not deeply beneath the casual humour, immensely proud, some would say absurdly proud of themselves? Was there is something in the name? The word Chilcotin is, by one definition, an attempt to say in English the aboriginal word for "River of The Young Men." They were there for a dream, the kind of dreams young men have and middle-aged men think they know better than to hang on to.

Of course it is good that Chilcotin has joined the rest of the world. A little different now, but no longer unique. It would be churlish not to rejoice for these people. But I will always be grateful that I knew Chilcotin when it was young, wild, funny and free, dreaming the glorious and impossible dreams that only youth knows.

BIG CREEK
October 14, 2000

This book has been exhaustively tested
for political correctness and is
certified to be uncontaminated.

Everything You Need
to Make a Ranch

ALEXIS CREEK—We were in a ranch-house kitchen the other night hunting for the bottom of a whisky bottle when the question came up of what you need to be a rancher today.

Health and brains we didn't count. It's never been proven the first is necessary and the second can actually be a handicap.

We threw out stamina, endurance, and ambition, too. Those are just brag subjects.

As for expanded knowledge of new ranching techniques, the hell with them. Most ranchers in Chilcotin aren't running their places as well as they already know how to.

Love of cows and horses didn't count. There wasn't a rancher present who would admit to anything more than a bare tolerance of either.

We decided it was time to be practical, to discuss the priorities, the way the prime minister advises us.

These emerged as the priorities for ranching today, listed in the order of their importance.

The first thing to get was a pickup truck. Fact is, it's getting hard to remember if there were ranchers before there were pickups.

The pickup should have power brakes and power steering, a deer-gun rack behind the seat, and Farm Vehicle written on the side. In the box there should be a broken jack, a bale of hay, and a dog. Almost any dog that barks will do.

The next important thing is an accountant, preferably a smart one.

This accountant's job is to understand most of the federal and provincial government regulations. He should be tested occasionally.

If the accountant interprets regulations correctly just 50 per cent of the time, he is only guessing and you could do as well yourself. Find one that can read the regulations right at least two times out of three.

You will need a good tax lawyer, too. He will explain why heavy losses are your only hope. That will fit right in with what you're doing. Give him a piece of the ranch from time to time.

You will need to know all you can about feed grain subsidies and the Crow's Nest Pass freight rates. Study them for a few years. If you get good at them, you can quit ranching and become chairman of the Canadian Transport Commission, which is indoor work with no heavy lifting.

A good banker is next.

Find one who doesn't understand anything about ranching. That won't be hard.

It would be best if you don't know anything about finance and cannot tell a demand note for $9\frac{1}{2}$ per cent from a Rinso soap coupon. That way you and your banker will start out even, which is only fair. You can grow up together.

 You will need a wife.

Find an attractive, intelligent, well-educated girl who likes carrying water in a pail and is happy to get laundry soap for a birthday present.

Raise a lot of kids. You will need the baby bonus to fix the pickup when they are young and you will find work for them to do from about the age of eight.

You will find the boys will work all right, up to the time they are old enough to pull the pin and head for Vancouver.

To keep the daughters cheerful, however, you will have to buy them at least one horse apiece, which they will spoil with love and cube sugar.

While you're at it, pick up some horses for yourself. They're not as handy as a plane or a motorcycle, but they sort of dress up the place.

Knowing your own ranch isn't enough; don't let yourself get cut off from the doings of the outside world. Buy a subscription to *Western Horseman*.

You will also need:

eighty-dollar boots;

a nickel-plated belt buckle;

some rope;

a set of moose horns for the living room wall, and

a cheque book.

Once you have put this all together you might try getting a cow and a bull together and see if anything happens.

Lessons from a
Swimming Eagle

FLETCHER LAKE—Inside Jack Tanner's cabin by the lakeside a drum heater is throwing out a good Chinook. It would be easy, over a whisky or two, to believe that life was going to be forever warm and rich, but we both knew that winter was driving down on Chilcotin. A lot of creatures living this day would not live to see the suns of next spring.

The coot was just one more proof that nature is not kind and that the great outdoor life we are supposed to call good and natural is red in tooth and claw.

Two male Bald Eagles had chosen that coot. They circled above him in a pewter grey sky and took turns drowning him. They'd been at it for some time, Jack said.

The coot was one of a few score pausing to rest for a few days along this shore of the lake before resuming their migration to the south. Each time the hunted coot rose to the surface, one or both of the eagles swooped down as if to grab him and he dove again. He can do this for a long time, but not indefinitely. Sooner or later the dives become shorter as his energy runs down and the eagles make sure he hasn't much time to grasp oxygen on the surface.

"They'll just wear him out, one after the other, until eventually he'll give up and one of them will fly across the lake to eat him with the other following so he can eat too," said Jack. He is a commercial fisherman from Sointula who spends autumns up here, hunting and observing little dramas like this one.

An odd feature of the contest is that the other coots of the flock have not fled to the far end of Fletcher Lake but continue nearby feeding, fighting and fooling in their usual way, unconcerned and unafraid. They can do this because everybody involved in this little action, the eagles, the coots and we humans, realize that the hunters have chosen their bird and no other creatures are in danger.

Biologists have observed this in wolves hunting moose and lions hunting zebras on the Serengeti Plain. There passes between the prey and the predator what is often called The Look. By the look, both sides agree to engage in the game of death. North American Indians sometimes reversed this well known and frequently observed aspect of predation, saying that it is the hunted that seeks out the hunter.

So the other coots kept feeding, just as the zebras continue to feed in Africa while one of their band is marked for death and left to face it alone. The eagles kept diving. The coot's time under the water grew shorter.

Jack and I could have interfered with nature's processes and saved the coot. We could probably have scared the eagles away by shouting, if not, then by firing shotguns near them so they could hear the whistle of shot going past. Why didn't we? Because if it wasn't this coot it would be another; also because the eagles weren't doing anything that we weren't doing in this country. They were hunting, as we were. The birds we took didn't suffer as much as the coot, but humans are expected to be humane. Eagles are only responsible for being eagles.

The moment came when the coot fluttered awkwardly before it could bring itself to dive again. It was exhausted. One of the eagles came down on the water, grabbed it as it went below and swam ashore with it.

Eagles are not supposed to be able to swim. They have no webs on their feet with which to paddle. Their feathers, unlike those of the coots and ducks, have no oil to repel water. Any eagle wet enough is a sodden, dead eagle.

"They can do it, though," said Jack, who has often watched them snatching salmon this way out of rivers on the coast. "Sometimes they grab a salmon that's too big for them and the fish pulls them under. They have to let go. People say they can't unhook their claws but they can. I've seen it happen."

But how does a bird with no swimming feet swim ashore? The eagle in front of us paddles in using his wings like oars, still holding the dying coot. He's out of his element, he's awkward, but he does it.

Ashore, standing on firm ground, triumphant, he's too wet and too tired to do anything more than stand there to dry out. His companion eagle grabs the coot and flies away with it. "Selfish bastard," said Jack.

Seeing the Neighbour's Light

BIG CREEK—What with making watches and banking, the Swiss people find themselves with a lot of money to spend, and a number of them are spending it in Chilcotin to buy house and land.

They say one was challenged to say why. "This may be beautiful country, but so is Switzerland. Why come all the way here to see the same thing?"

"Look out my front window," said the Switzer. "Tell me what you see."

The questioner looked. "I see a lake, grass and trees."

"Look more. Look closer. What do you see?"

"The lake, which is blue. The pines which are green. The poplar trees which are yellow. The grass that is brown. Mountain peaks which are white. Blue sky. White clouds."

"But tell me, what else do you see?"

"I see nothing else. Lake, forest, mountains. That's all."

"Exactly," said the Switzer.

His children, however, aren't likely to have such a view from their front window in Big Creek. The country is filling up.

This old ranch settlement is on the verge of being within commuting distance of Williams Lake, a small city which offers the jobs and the amenities usual to small cities anywhere.

There is another factor in play at the turn of this century. The Internet and all the attendant technology has made it possible for many city workers to take their office home. Provided there is a touch-tone telephone connection it doesn't much matter whether your office is in a log cabin in the bush or downtown Vancouver.

Big Creek still has dial phones, the new symbol of frontier life. It irritates them since they have been on line since 1913. That will change.

Nobody foresaw how The Chip would change society, and most of us still have not perceived even where we are now on that long technologic road. However, we already know that there is no need for an office worker to go to his office.

No one even dreamed of the Internet when I first saw Big Creek. Then, and for decades after, the virtue of this country was the isolation it offered—privacy, if you prefer another word. The ranches were so far apart that every man had to keep his own tom cat and nobody could see the lights of a neighbour's house at night.

Nobody cared particularly about the cats' sex lives, but not being able to see the neighbour's lights at night was the standard of the good life. For a diminishing number of people here, it still is.

One fall I set up a trailer camp for the hunting season in a friend's back pasture. Of course I could not see the house nor could they see me. That natural modesty was taken for granted.

However, I stayed late that year and as November neared the ranch wife remarked that now that the leaves had blown off the poplar trees, she could see the propane light with which I lit the trailer by night. Next year I moved farther away where the fall of autumn leaves would not leave us naked in one another's sight.

The Old West.

"Good clean air from east to west/And room to go and come/I love my fellow man the best/When he is scattered some."

There are still a dozen families here who cannot see the neighbour's lights at night and a few are far enough from the main roads that they still go to the window when they hear a truck engine to see who is travelling. Probably not many have paused to think that in most of the world, this situation is as remote from today's realities as the Crusades.

In almost all Europe you cannot even escape the sound of human voices by night, let alone the light in the neighbour's window. Asians have a tendency to huddle, whether in the big tiger economy cities such as Singapore or in tiny villages where there isn't any electricity to light the lamps. Mexicans take comfort in the presence of other Mexicans either by day or by night. Most of the world sets no great store by isolation, and a large part tries frantically to avoid it.

So, perhaps, do now the Canadians.

We are clustered into a few large cities on the 49th Parallel where we are accustomed to being close enough to neighbours to smell their cooking and count their orgasms.

The politically correct sociologists—is there any other kind?—are hell-bent on herding us into city tenements and forcing us to give up our cars and our tiny bit of independence from the Almighty State.

The Switzer identified the reality.

"Nothing but trees and mountains? Now you know why I left Switzerland."

Seeking the Sound of Silence

BIG CREEK—In the gloaming, that lovely time between day and night, we were all in camp talking in low voices about nothing much and lowering the level in the Glenlivet jar. The youngest man present, Mexican born, American raised, said, "Excuse me please, I am going over and sit on that old snake fence for a while."

Why, we said.

"I want to listen to the silence," he said. "In all my life, this is the only place I ever heard it."

He left and sat on the fence for a while. We others listened, too, to the silence. It is precious stuff and there's less of it around than there used to be. Each man thought of the time when he first encountered it.

Mine was also here in this corner of Chilcotin. I was waiting for a night flight of ducks beside Mons Creek on the edge of the darkness when I heard a faint whisper, a shish, shish, shish. So faint as to be at the extreme limit of hearing. After a while, I found that it matched my pulse rate and then I realized that for the first time I was hearing tiny hairs inside my ears moving against each other to the beat of my pulse. That was the closest I ever came to hearing silence.

True silence is, of course, the stuff of dreams. Like a vacuum, it is a quality of outer space where the music of the spheres is silence. On earth silence is a concept rather than a reality, a condition we can approach by scientific instruments but can never fully achieve. It truly exists only for a minuscule number of human beings whose nerve connections between ears and brain are severed. The famous Helen Keller, who overcame total deafness and blindness, said in her later years that if she could have had only one faculty, that would have been hearing.

Everybody else, including those who call themselves stone deaf, hear a bit of something most of the time.

If perfect silence may never be known to almost all of us, men remain intrigued by the idea and like to tell themselves, from time to time, that they have found it.

Our friend on the old, grey fence in the late russet skylight thought he had found it, but he had spent his childhood amid the ceaseless noise of a Mexican village: cocks crowing, dogs barking, tractor motors, the ever-present hum of human voices, children crying, music playing and the seabirds crying. Even in the nights when men were sleeping all sorts of birds and reptiles of the darkness spoke strangely of things which men do not know. Los Angeles, where he later lived, was the kingdom of the automobile, the whine of tires and the mutter of motors part of the very fabric of life, and over that the blare of radio and television, the whine of jet motors, all those clatters, bangs and thumps of modern society which reduce the hearing of the average individual by one per cent per year throughout his lifetime.

Here in Chilcotin, in this hour after the sun had left the sky, he had found a place so quiet he believed it was soundless.

On this evening in this place he could have heard the rustle from the creek, which ran past almost a kilometre distant. The high yelps of a family of coyotes, even farther away, could be heard well enough to be identified. And on the same thin edge of hearing was the bump, bump, bumbumbumbumbump of a male grouse drumming for his lady love, fanning the air with his wings moving so fast he broke the sound barrier with them.

19

"Very beautiful," said the young man from Mexico. "Very beautiful, the silence."

Others have said it the same, at greater length.

Robert Service, bard of the Yukon, wrote:

"It's the great big broad land 'way up yonder/It's the forests where silence has lease/It's the beauty that fills me with wonder,/It's the stillness that fills me with peace."

And the prophet Isiah may have been saying much the same in Chapter 5, Verse 8:

"Woe be unto them that join house to house, that lay field to field, till there be no place that they may be placed alone in the midst of life."

Alas, a Land Not Fit
for Camp Robbers

BIG CREEK—There is good news and there is bad news from the Chilcotin Country. Here's the good news first. This land is filled with wild creatures as seldom before.

We see moose less often than in the Fifties, but they are still here despite all that the in-season and out-of-season shooters can do. Deer are numerous enough to become a road hazard, and more people now put deer-warning whistles on the front fender.

Black bears, who apparently have lots to eat without chewing up humans, clown around on the roadsides and in the forest. There's a murmurous crowd of ducks on every pothole, loons calling on the lakes, geese honking about everything and nothing, as usual.

On nearby Big Flat dwells a Sandhill Crane which must be at least a metre and a half tall, for his eye level is almost at that of a human.

Tall, erect, slender, with a long nose, he resembles a British upper-class snob in another less appealing way—he contrives to indicate that the people here do not measure up to his expectations. However, he is a spectacle worth seeing. When he flies his wings look like two sheets of four-by-eight plywood waving.

Last night, as alternate entertainment, a beaver appeared on the road in front of the car, galloping toward us. When we stopped, he passed close enough to be touched, paying us not the slightest attention. He was at least two kilometres from the nearest water, so probably his parents had kicked him out of the lodge in which he was born and grew up and told him to go out into the world and write when he found work.

In camp here, the hummingbird feeder hums all the daylight hours, and the tube that holds wild bird seed has attracted juncos in the dozens. (They may be White Crowned Sparrows, or maybe Pine Grosbeaks, or perhaps Townsend's Solitaires. I am sure they are birds.)

With all this good news, how can there be bad news?

Well, there is. There isn't a Whiskey Jack to be found.

Come to think of it, there weren't any Whiskey Jacks in camp last fall and during the winter, when we trudged in through the snow, none came. We nail chunks of suet to the poplar, but they stay until age withers them and we bait again with another piece.

Bait Whiskey Jacks?

Whiskey Jacks used to show up as soon as you pulled a chunk of slab bacon out of the grub box, demanding the first piece. Camp Robbers is one of their names. Canada Jay is another. They needed no coaxing. They are bold, brave little bandits who invite themselves to every social event in the wilderness.

More than one became bold enough to snatch bits of fat from between my teeth. You could regularly feed them by hand on a day or two's acquaintance.

Somehow you never minded that they helped themselves to anything and everything that they fancied. They were such delightful little creatures, dove grey with brushmarks of white and an eye bright and black as a shoe button. Like other members of the crow family, intelligent but, unlike the crows, cuddly.

We miss them the way the Biblical father missed the prodigal son and would cheerfully serve some fatted calf if they'd just come back again.

It's time to call on an expert, and the best expert is P. A. Taverner, famed author of *Western Birds*. He notes that Jays are not above stealing such things as beer bottle caps, which don't matter, and engagement rings, which do, but he notes, with his usual accuracy, "Few wild things have as many human friends."

Then Mr. Taverner proceeds to speak the unspeakable, the awful, the dreadful truth about our saucy friends. Hear this:

"The jay shrinks from civilization. *As soon as the temporary camp becomes a permanent settlement it deserts the area.*" (Emphasis ours.)

The bad news hits like a hard drive to the family jewels. This isn't a matter of a saucy little bird leaving us; it's the reason for his leaving that is appalling. This country has become too civilized to be fit for Whiskey Jacks.

Even though most of us think civilization is far from here and something for other people to worry about, the wise little bird has smelt it creeping up on us.

First blacktop and hydro, then Colonel Sanders fried chicken, government inspectors, protest marches and boom boxes.

So the Whiskey Jack is pulling out of this country, perhaps to make his final, impudent little stand up in the hills with the crust on the top.

It's dreadful. It's terrible. I can't write about it any more.

Poplars Rustle, Pines Sigh

Old Man Turner was so deaf that it was pretty well agreed all over West Chilcotin that if the Last Trump sounded, somebody would have to ride over to his cabin on Charlotte Lake and give him a swift boot so he would know.

Legend says that one night a big pine tree jumped out and hit the Model A Ford in which he and some others were drinking and that the accident restored Old Man Turner's hearing. A doctor at Williams Lake took the opportunity to tell him that if he wanted to keep his miraculously restored hearing he would have to quit drinking. After a while, however, he returned to Peaches Wine and other brews of the country because, he said, he liked what he'd been drinking a lot better than what he was now hearing.

I was taught to not contradict my elders, but Old Man Turner was wrong. Getting your hearing back is better than drinking. Not a lot better than Highland Malt Whisky, but better. I know because I have hearing aids stuck in both ears now and I wouldn't be without the things.

My hearing began to fade almost twenty years ago and about fifteen years ago I went to a doctor for testing. He found that I had lost 25 per cent of my hearing in the higher notes but, being one of the last of the male chauvinist pigs, he told me that to fail to hear a quarter of what my wife said to me was no handicap and to go away and be happy.

It got worse, and I was beginning to miss sounds like dinner bells and the punchlines of jokes.

Recent testing showed that I was picking up sound not all that shabbily, but I couldn't sort it out, having trouble (still) with the female voice and being unable to identify p, d, t, and other short sounds. Trying to distinguish between words like pet and met, tun and pun, tat and pat, I scored only 74 where, my tester said, I was getting enough sound to have scored 95 to 98.

Exactly. That is what causes people to think you are a card short of a full deck.

I can feel in my heart, even more than in my head, for the people, particularly the children, whose deafness is not diagnosed and who are categorized as dull, a situation far more common than most people or even most parents realize.

The trouble with the old hearing aids was that they merely amplified sounds for you. "You get confused more audibly," said the hearing specialist. The space age came to our rescue.

In communicating with satellites, scientists developed a system which aids the high-note-low-note deafness victim. Today's technology can reduce my hearing of low notes until it is at the same level as my hearing of high notes. The earpiece then raises both audibilities simultaneously, so that I am almost returned to normal hearing. Almost. You never get all the way back in this, in bifocal lenses, or in sex using Viagra.

Imperfect as it may be, it has returned me to a world I had almost forgotten. I name just a few rediscoveries:

I didn't know the river could be heard from my campsite in Chilcotin. It can. It rustles, day and night, a lovely sound.

The wind makes leafy trees rustle and pine trees sigh. I had forgotten.

I hear clocks tick again and remember childhood when I could hear the tick of a grandfather clock in the hall from my bedroom. (Until now, I didn't know that the quartz wall clocks could tick.)

The air is filled with birdsong. It's as if Rachel Carson had never lived, a situation many of us wish were true.

If you have hearing and don't hear birds, maybe you've stopped listening. Try doing earplugs for a while and then you will experience the glory when you hear them again.

There are also the silly little sounds, less important than birds and rivers, but part of the fabric of life we deaf people have not touched for too long. Bacon sizzling. The whir of an owl's wing at night. The clatter of mah jong coming out an open door in Chinatown. Phone lines humming at thirty below.

The industry makes a great to-do about creating hearing aids which are almost invisible. No thanks. Give me visible ones. Far better than saying, "Sorry, I have a hearing problem," to everybody you meet. They can see for themselves.

One more great thing: When afflicted with crashing bores, who have experienced a population explosion during my years of deafness, you can pretend to adjust the aid in one ear and then the other and turn them off.

Chilcotin Wears Laceup Shoes

BIG CREEK—Logging has done many good things for Chilcotin. Better roads, better services, more money to spend and more things to spend it on, better health care, better schools, better, better, better, better.

If things are so good, why aren't people here happier?

There is plenty of evidence that their material lives are better, but evidence that they are happier is harder to find.

Something is missing such as, for instance, when fat little Sammy Barrowman, owner of the log cabin Alexis Creek Hotel, which he claimed had the only flush toilets between Williams Lake and Yokohama, played Santa Claus one Christmas and was laid out cold when a kid hit his head with an orange. It was one of the first Mandarins ever seen in Chilcotin and frozen hard as a regulation baseball, of course. The presents that year were ball point pens, one of the very few things in which Chilcotin had contrived to come abreast of the dazzlingly new postwar age. When the kid who threw the orange came up, Santa Claus snapped the ballpoint pen in half before handing it to him.

What's this got to do with a region's happiness level? Nothing, perhaps, but it has something to do with regional spirit and spirit is part of being happy.

A few years ago when you were in Chilcotin, and it took a long time on the old roads and trails, you knew you were somewhere like no other place on earth. In these patched grasslands and forests the rivers raced through as clean as the morning of Creation. Independence was the key word. Not only was Chilcotin largely independent of the uncaring outside world, within Chilcotin every man was largely independent of every other man, neighbourly help excepted.

Many people went out, as it was said, just once a year to see the doctor and the banker at Williams Lake, quite confident that one day was enough to clear up any problems for the next twelve months.

The lifeline for supplies was the freight truck called The Stage, operated alternately by Red McCue and Squeak Wilson.

Once Squeak delivered a case of whisky to a Bella Coola store with one bottle opened and partly emptied. The store man beat the air and shouted that before he used The Stage again, hell would freeze solid from shore to shore and even then he was pre-pared to sit around on the ice for a while.

"Fair enough," said Squeak, "but since we aren't going to meet any more, let's have one more drink together for old time's sake." He unscrewed the cap of the broached cargo and they both had a drink.

There were two emergency cabins on the lonely road between Tatla and Anahim Lakes and the travellers, who were rare as pelicans in winter, counted their miles as they passed them in case they had to walk back to one to avoid freezing to death that night.

There was adventure for all, but there were limitations also.

You wonder how many mute, inglorious Miltons are today working the green chain at one of the Williams Lake sawmills because their education was in a ranch house kitchen.

How much of our memory of the good old days is nostalgia?

Nostalgia is like peeing your pants when lost in a blizzard. It gives a warm, comfortable feeling but that doesn't last and it's no real help.

Yes, there was much wrong, including things people prefer to not remember: insanity, crime, brutality, incest, all the sins. But sins continue and now without that sort of glory to life in the Chilcotin Country. Just by being there, people proved they were survivors, and although they occasionally lost their limbs or their lives they never lost their sense of humour.

They had, here, something greater than mere prosperity.

The Ritual Drunkups

WILLIAMS LAKE—On a Stampede week, the desk clerk at the Lakeview Hotel greeted one guest in the bright and friendly manner of the Lakeview people, saying, "You look a little bit drunk this morning."

He was a big man, cow boss of the gang, and he came to the counter and planked there two hands the size of Missouri Hams. "Young lady," he said, "if I am not drunk I have just wasted five hundred dollars and a week of my time."

That was years ago. People in Chilcotin don't drink the way they used to. They drink more often now, but they do it in moderation and seem to enjoy it less. Old timers knew that in taking alcohol, a little excess is called for. Or, as the old chief said when asked by the fur trader how big a drink he wanted, "A little too much is just enough."

Yes, it's true, some people's lives are ruined by alcohol, so it should be wrong to write columns encouraging people to use it, but then it's also wrong for governments to push alcohol and gambling. But they do that and rake in money by the hundreds of millions of dollars every year by doing it. This column won't pay hundreds of millions of dollars. It's written, partly, for fun and with fond memories.

Chilcotin long had a reputation for heavy drinking which

wasn't deserved. There were a few alcoholics who drank themselves into illness and the grave, but it's doubtful the ratio of
hopeless drunks to general population was as high as it was in
West Vancouver. Most people, rich and poor, experienced long
periods of alcohol drought here and did not complain about it.

Their idea was, if you are going to drink, do a job of it. Make
sure everybody knows you are drunk. As one cowboy who once
a year used to take the biggest beef drive into Williams Lake put
it, "It's hardly worthwhile starting unless you got a case of it
on hand."

Drinking was more a ritual than a social habit.

The old prospector, driven out of the hills with the crust on top
by the winter, would find a cabin, a case and, usually, an old dog
for company, and he would drink until it was all gone. He would
have a terrible hangover but would say that it was worth it. The
drinking over, he would start eating again, purged of whatever
devils had been hounding him in the months of summer. He might
not take another sip for a year.

Other drinkers took hotel rooms, from which they did not
emerge for many long days. What little food they took was left at
their door.

The more convivial found kindred spirits, and all went on a
great drunkup together, leaving humour and tragedy, the two
accompaniments of alcohol and the theatre, in their wake.

Such a cluster of drinkers would migrate from house to house
through such towns as Williams Lake. Sooner or later everybody
got to know where the drunk was located today and would visit
and knock off a few themselves.

It was then no disgrace to be drunk. It wasn't any great honour, either. It was a ritual which those not partaking could never-
theless observe with respect and refrain from interrupting.

The country objected only to mean drunks. A small fist fight
was acceptable, provided it was between friends, but nothing
more violent was permissible. Those who used alcohol to rid

themselves of unforgivable things they wished to say to friends and relatives soon found themselves with nobody to talk to.

It was predominantly a male pastime, like bird shooting and fixing truck engines. In this age when women are demanding equality in everything it wouldn't fit well because, with all due respect, very few women are capable of good drunks. There is something missing in their brains. They were, however, tolerant and even more.

A favourite memory is an Anahim Lake Stampede and a rancher who was hard working, honest, God fearing, sincere and all round decent. He had everything a man should have except happiness.

He was missing when a few us were sitting around his camp fire, where his wife was cooking fried meat for us. One of the fruit of his loins came up out of the darkness and said, "Hey, Mum. Dad is getting drunked up."

"Isn't that great," she said, "I'm so glad. Your father doesn't get drunk as often as he deserves."

On that inevitable day, now probably not far off, when our sanctimonious British Columbia government piously sues the distillery industry for forcing it to sell all that highly profitable poison to the public, it need not look this way for a supporting witness.

Ode to Godawful Roads

ANAHIM LAKE—The greatest roadbuilders the world has known since the Romans are the British Columbia loggers, and some people here say they have damn nigh ruined Chilcotin.

Of course there are others here who welcome good roads. As far as they are concerned, if the loggers want to follow other old Roman ways and toss the odd virgin to the lions, that form of rodeoing is okay with them provided they have the roads which enable them to drive the BMW to Boitano Mall in Williams Lake every Friday night.

It's not only the loggers who are building highways. Loggers build 80 km/h forest access roads which now cover the face of the Chilcotin plateau like the roots of some monstrously large fir tree. But they aren't alone. The government is doing it too. The government, always the damnable government.

Government crews are straightening corners, chopping off hills and smearing blacktop over half the country. You can drive into Chilcotin and out of Chilcotin so fast you may never be entirely sure you were here.

Government made the Becher's Prairie stretch so good that now it has to hire policemen with radar detectors to arrest people who use the road the way the engineers intended. First you give the kid ice cream, then you slap it out of the little beggar's hand because it is fattening and he should know better than to eat it.

Progress.

Whether good roads are for better or for worse, for richer or for poorer, is hard to determine, as many people find out after getting married. Of one thing we can have no doubt. Things are never going to be the same again here.

The Chilcotin Country change is irreversible and possibly terminal.

Blacktop roads have brought a different element into the country, people with shiny laceup shoes who wash their cars every week and have commitments to whales. They have caught up with, perhaps passed, those who came into Chilcotin to get away from people like them.

So how were things, really, in the good and bad days of old, when earth was young and all the rivers here were stiff with trout?

Most people took two days instead of four hours to drive from Williams Lake to Anahim Lake. That's one change.

In the winter, most people didn't try it. For those who did, there were emergency cabins, one near Kleena Kleene and the other near Cariboo Flat, where a man with truck trouble could avoid freezing to death on a winter's night, although barely.

Not far from One Eye Lake were the Sand Hills. To cross them you closed your eyes and floored it. I did this once and bent fenders with a downhill man who, because he was stopped, became the innocent party. These days such a collision would cost a thousand dollars or so and loss of points in the ICBC computer, but things were different then. I promised to pay him ten dollars, which, then as now, was about the real cost of his damage, and he loaned me some shotgun ammunition of which I had run short. Neither of us had ever met before or heard the other's name. Bad road made us brothers.

In those days before ambulance chasing, we knew nothing of

that extraordinarily profitable insurance company ailment called whiplash, which has since provided lifetime incomes for so many British Columbians.

Yes, we were far different people.

At the top of the McClinchy Hill was the Boulder Patch. Much of the road from the lake was made of boulders about the size of your fist or at least no bigger than grapefruit. Atop the McClinchy Hill was a stretch where the smallest was the size of a regulation soccer ball. This was where two-man vehicles proved their value.

The passenger would walk in front of the car, pointing right or left to where the wheel should be placed so that the entire bowel system of the vehicle was not left strewn on the rocks. Crossing the Boulder Patch was best done before you drank too much Road Straightener. We drank Road Straightener in those days too.

You may say, what good came of the Sand Hills, the Boulder Patch and the many horrors you haven't yet gone on and on about?

Gentle Jesus,

Sweet and mild,

Watch and keep thee,

Little child.

They were good because they filtered the people who came to Chilcotin. Those who couldn't face bog holes, sand traps and rock piles turned back and drove to Kelowna or White Rock where they could be among their own kind, and a good thing too, because they would never have fitted in here.

Now, progress has seized Chilcotin by the throat and is shaking it. Oh well.

Bad Roads Built Character

An umbrage taker in Anahim Lake has taken the usual dose about a recent column concerning Chilcotin roads. She says good roads are necessary in times of sickness and accident, and I shouldn't criticize them. Dear lady, I enjoy them too. Use them, all the time. Even got a speeding ticket, which used to be only theoretically possible in Chilcotin.

Goodness was not the point of the column and, since you insist, perhaps mercy shouldn't be either. So let's be blunt. Good roads have eroded the moral fibre of the Chilcotin Country.

Do good roads build character? Answer: no.

I note you refer to the stretch between Anahim Lake and Bella Coola as bad road. This suggests to me that you are of a generation which subscribes to the legend that you need a four wheel drive to manage the big hill. If the valley people can keep that legend alive, good luck to them, they'll keep their privacy a while longer. However, it was never true. I can testify to that. I was there the day it opened, about fifty years ago, driving an ordinary car.

But different times bring different views. There are now a great many British Columbians, not all of them in Vancouver, whose measure of a road emergency is that they have to call B.C. Automobile Association on their cell phone.

Things were much different here. There was, for instance, the case of the Englishman whose car broke down—and who had a car which did not break down on those wicked old roads?—on a cold winter's night. He froze to death.

Injuries? Strange as it may sound today, the idea that frontier British Columbians have a right to hospital care, telephones and good roads is a recent development.

Ask Dave Dorsey of your community of Anahim Lake, who still limps. Forty years ago when he broke his leg they tried moving him in a wagon, but the pain was too much for any rapid travel. It was two days before he got medical attention in Williams Lake. Nobody thought much about it at the time, except to say, "Tough goin', eh Dave?"

Chilcotin may be the country which originated the saying "See you Sunday, God willing and the creeks don't rise."

No sensible person, and not many of the other kinds of person, started a road journey with any certainty of when it would end. Countless were stuck in bog holes overnight during spring breakup, waiting for anything human to come along in anything that ran. Often nobody came along and half the next day, beginning in the cold first light of dawn, was spent jacking up the vehicle and building corduroy road underneath it with jack pine.

If somebody came along, he sometimes ended up stuck also. Misery loves company. Nobody drove past a stuck car, however. In those days people would throw horse buns at anybody who passed a stalled vehicle without asking if help was needed.

Most people learned to make the accursed thing run, somehow.

Just one of a thousand examples: the Ross brothers of Pemberton who came up into the Shulaps Mountains of Chilcotin to hunt sheep and tore out their transmission near the summit. In three days they stripped out the transmission, rejigged it and, jamming in a strip of metal cut from a one quart oil can, locked it into one gear which brought them out of the mountains to home.

The idea of summoning help was beyond insanity. They had

no summoning equipment, and anyway hardly anybody in British Columbia knew where the Shulaps are.

Some cars and trucks lose 20 per cent of their value by being driven out of a showroom. Cars and trucks sold into old Chilcotin lost just about everything. Who wanted to buy a second-hand Chilcotin vehicle? Few makes could survive the pounding for long, and the International, which proved to be one survivor, was honoured with the nickname Intersmashable.

Road signs, hand lettered, were eloquent.

CHOOSE YOUR RUT WITH CARE,
YOU'LL BE IN IT FOR 15 MILES.

PROCEED WITH CAUTION,
LIKE PORCUPINES MAKE LOVE.

This did not produce a race of auto mechanics. The average Chilcotin resident lost half the nuts and most of the springs off anything he took apart to repair, and the fact that vehicles kept running had more to do with God than man. But bad roads produced a hardy, confident and strangely cheerful breed of people.

They would drive anything anywhere they thought they saw two tire tracks cutting into the jack pine curtain, and when they ended up high centred in the loon, too bad. They couldn't stage a protest parade, the roads weren't fit to march on.

Getting Lost is Half the Fun

BIG CREEK—One thing some of us thought would be with us for as long as the trees grow and the rivers flow: that natural human right to lose our way in the great northern forest. Everyone who has spent time in the bush has experienced that adrenaline rush and been improved by it.

It's not that you don't know where you are. You know exactly where you are. You are standing among a bunch of trees, every one of which looks just about like every other one. What you do not know is where everything else in the world is. This is the stuff of which stories are born.

The late Bennie Abbott of Williams Lake, when he was new to the Cariboo Country, went hunting with a companion near 83 Mile and couldn't find his car, or even the road the car was parked on. He and the partner searched until the shadows of evening grew and decided their only course was to build a fire, sit over it all night and wait for rescue in the morning.

"Then we heard a truck motor," said Bennie. "We decided we would wait until the noise grew louder and then fainter, and at that point, the road must be closest to us and we would walk in that direction.

"The motor noise got louder and louder. Eventually we could

see Hodgson Brothers written on the side of the freight truck, which almost ran over us. We had been about to make camp twenty feet off the side of the road."

This is one of the classic tales, but each of us can list our own. I once lost an automobile, not in the forest but on a hillside which had been clear cut and was as open as the surface of the moon. Hunting for Sharptail Grouse, I had turned and watched the car, from time to time, shining in the morning sun. Then it went and could not be found again, as is the way it happens.

Since all cut-over forestlands have roads in the shape of trees, I followed one branch to the main trunk and walked the trunk road to public highway, then slowly, wearily returned and found the car before nightfall. The car hadn't moved.

Neither did my car move itself on another occasion when I parked it by a roadside and walked to the right into some heavy timber and returned twenty minutes later to find it where I left it but facing the wrong way. The only way this phenomenon could seem to occur was that I had walked across the road. To this day I can't remember doing it. And I wasn't even frightened that day.

You may say someone who can get lost in such circumstances can get lost in a phone booth. You may be right. But I am not alone.

Old Daniel Boone had it right when he told the lady that in all his long life on the frontier he had never once been lost, but he was once bewildered for five days.

Most of us have been bewildered for hours, and a few of us overnight. It is as natural as headaches and the common cold and sometimes more fun.

There have been tragic cases. The traveller who walks a few feet into the forest to urinate, gets turned around and is found miles away, dead of exhaustion and hypothermia two days later.

There are other cases such as the 11 year old Cariboo boy who was thrown from his horse and lost in the woods for six days. He never panicked, he conserved his strength, he calmly took a direction and kept it, knowing that sooner or later any direction will bring you to civilization. He saved himself by walking out while scores were searching for him.

The secret is to be, like Daniel Boone, not frightened into panicky action merely because you are bewildered for a while. Anyone, except toddlers, can remember to carry a good knife, matches and a whistle. At worst, you can build a fire and sit beside it waiting to be found.

Once you lose the terror, which happens after the first time or two, it adds spice to the day's menu. It becomes a small, safe adventure.

Except for an outfit called Magellan Systems which advertises a Ground Position System, operating on a little hand-held device which reads signals from a satellite. "Store up to 100 hard-to-find hunting and fishing spots in its memory and it will direct you to them, any time, in any weather, anywhere in the world."

Somehow I don't think I am going to buy one.

Trees of Ivory and Gold

BIG CREEK—Although I call the poplar grove my own it doesn't belong to me, but then, the whole idea that trees or the land belong to anybody is just a human conceit. All anybody does is make camp for a while as we pass through.

I have camped in this grove, off and on, for many years, know all its trees and, if I lack ownership, I do have a strong moral claim to the place.

Now, in the summer days, the leaves whisper sweet nothings by day and there are birds to sing, squirrels to talk and, by night, an old owl who hoots musically and flies overhead like a great moth, his wings soft on the air.

I have seen these trees in the thin, short days of winter when the cold air stalks down on this country from the Arctic. Perhaps it is imagination, but the trunks of the poplars seem more grey than white in the winter. The wood is brittle, and a passing moose, if he chews off a few boughs, will crunch them like pretzels. In one corner of the grove an ice storm struck a few springs ago and the weight bowed some trees until their tips almost touched the ground. A couple of them never stood upright again.

Spring is when the dark, brown sticky sap oozes from the poplar's buds, the fragrant stuff we call Balm of Gilead.

Autumn is their glory time. Some mysterious clock tells their leaves to turn brilliant yellow. The process is normally attributed to frosts, but since at this elevation there are frosts every month of the year, the explanation is obviously not a complete one. Few sights can rival a poplar grove in September, the tree trunks pillars of ivory holding aloft golden clouds of leaves.

Most of northern Canada and Siberia are an almost seamless carpet of coniferous forests—pines in the drier lands and spruce elsewhere. The poplar in its various forms is islanded in these forests. In the poplar groves the grass grows beneath the trees, there are mushrooms, wild onions, purple asters and a host of other small and delicate plants which, for all their frailty, have survived in these lands since the ice age ended ten thousand years ago.

Poplars ring most of our lakes, ponds and isolated meadows. The human, walking the dark and featureless pine forest, is often guided from meadow to meadow to lake by sighting on poplar stands.

Poplars are a large family of trees in the northern lands and include the huge cottonwoods that grow in the river bottoms. Purists point out that what Cariboo and Chilcotin people call white poplar is a poplar variety properly called aspen. But most of us don't heed purists. We call bison buffalo, we call wapiti elk, and we'll call aspen poplar if we choose.

A thousand ranch kids have carved their initials in poplar bark and been able to read the letters, etched in black, when they are middle aged. About 1972, waiting for a night flight of ducks in a grove beside a lake here, I marked in the tree BORING, ISN'T IT? You can still read it, together with the YES! some other hunter added.

We know poplar makes good firewood, if split soon after falling and burned within 18 months. Fewer of us know that it makes beautiful wood panelling which, unlike pine panelling, does not go yellow and orange with age. In all the Cariboo, only the Linde Brothers on the Dog Creek road still mill the snow-white, red-streaked groove-and-tongue poplar boards which customers line up a year ahead of time to buy. It's cranky wood to use, but one of the most beautiful once it's on the walls.

Mike Carson of B.C. Forestry Department says these trees are the most underrated crop in all B.C. Although up in Fort Nelson the world's largest chopstick factory uses poplar, most commercial operations have little use for it. But those are mere financial considerations. They have no place in my private grove where, when a rain storm is bearing down upon us, the trees give the first warning by showing the underside of their leaves.

Like most old country stories, the Quaking Aspen signal has a basis in fact. You can observe that the leaves do not turn upside down; they are tossed about by gusty, erratic winds. It often does mean rain, because such winds usually accompany an advancing low pressure front. One may, of course, prefer to believe that spirits live in this lovely glade with us and that, like us, they like to see the trees dancing from time to time.

The Lady Hunts Sheep

HANCEVILLE—When little Heidi became a Class B game guide the first hunter assigned to her said, "Just my luck. I get a girl for a guide."

"Just my luck to get a jerk like you," she said. "But we're stuck with one another, so let's get on with it."

She found a legal ram for him and that improved matters. He was an American and wildly competitive.

She says she likes most of the hunters she takes out. Most are Americans. Before their currency collapsed, there were a few Mexicans. "It's a chance to hear somebody talking some sense. You don't hear much sense down here in the South."

She guides out of Telegraph Creek in B.C.'s big, empty northwest quarter, has her own outfit and charges a round thousand dollars a day per customer to hunt this most elusive, most remote, most exciting of all the ordinary big game animals. Sheep are rare trophies, and even experienced hunters sometimes pursue them for several years without ever getting a legal ram in the sights of their gun.

Heidi is by no means the first woman to become a big game guide in B.C. Gerry Bracewell of Tatla Lake was guiding two generations before Heidi was a gleam in her father's eye. What

45

distinguishes Heidi is her fee, which is quite a bit above the ordinary for sheep hunts.

"Grizzly bear hunts are cheaper, $850 a day usually, but for a sheep hunt I want $14,000 for a two week hunt. I get it because people know that what I promise, I deliver.

"When the hunters come I don't have any stories about this horse going lame or that pack saddle being broken. I'm ready. They've got a right to expect that and I spend a lot of money on my equipment. The word gets around. I get almost all my hunters by word-of-mouth advertising."

She keeps two homes, one in Telegraph Creek and one on a chunk of the original Hance ranch here in Chilcotin, a place which Vancouver people call North but which she knows to be in the South. Here she winters the horses. In some recent years she has also run a trap line here during the winters, but that was before the ecofreaks ruined the fur market.

She was born Heidi Gutfrucht in Vancouver and raised on a little swamp hay ranch in the Davis Lake area. Her father ran a small herd but also worked out, as is the lot of so many small ranchers. There is very little about horses, cows, cold weather, privation and guns that she does not know. Although she is small and slim she has big, wide square hands.

As a child, and even more now, horses fill a good part of her life. "I like horses. But I'm not like some women. Some women really like them and want to go barrel racing and to shows and so forth. If I'm going to use a horse, I have got to have a mission." In other words, second class riding is better than first class walking.

Her first guiding mission was for Sherwood Henry in the Whitewater country. Later she went north to guide for a Telegraph Creek outfit and fortuitously and unexpectedly inherited $20,000 from a great-aunt in Germany just in time to buy into a partnership there.

She has since bought out the other partner and now operates

the outfit with her daughter, Echo, who has an assistant guide's licence and, unlike Heidi, a college degree as well.

Her success rate in hunting sheep?

Almost all guides wince at that question. It's like asking how much money you have in the bank. It's not really polite, but, then, newspapermen are seldom polite. In her usual, direct way, she doesn't blink at it. What's in the mind comes out the mouth.

"In 15 years I had two hunters fail to get their ram. One of them quit the hunt on me. In the other case, I got weathered out in the mountains."

She will celebrate her fortieth birthday in those northern mountains this August, chasing a Stone thinhorn sheep with two customers (two per guide is the limit) in her assigned territory near the Stikine River Valley. From base camp they will have ridden saddle horses for two days and walked and climbed for another two. "I'll be at my fighting weight, which is 150. I'm 155 now."

With two grand a day from two guests, is she going to be wealthy some day?

"Nope. Not wealthy. Too many expenses. But I will be comfortable."

You wonder if Heidi will be happy when comfortable. Comfort is not exactly what sheep hunters choose.

How a Hello Girl Goes Hiking

BIG CREEK—The Chilcotin Country has always had its own particular set of heroes, and if they aren't recognized as heroes by the rest of the world, then the rest of the world would have to take out its imagination and gallop it full out to reach even a faint appreciation of how little the people of Chilcotin care about the opinion of the rest of the world.

One of the Chilcotin heroes is a former Hello Girl named Janet Elizabeth Rhodes. She has gone where few frontier people go, and she has walked every foot of it, alone.

But before telling about her epic footslogs, a little history for people too young to know what Hello Girls were. They were also known as Central and it was a sad day for us all when the telephone companies changed over to those recordings which say "Press 3 for Swahili, Press 1 if you didn't pay, Press 6 and get lost." That we permitted big companies to rob us of those friendly, intelligent and helpful Hello Girls is just one more proof that Canadians are wimps and deserve to get kicked around.

Janet saw the end of her helpful trade looming after service in her native Nanaimo, in Victoria and in Williams Lake. She quit to become a cook on Dick Church's ranch in Big Creek, which was a challenge because at the time she couldn't cook. The Churches were good about it, and she became a very good cook. She is now manager of the cafeterias at Williams Lake and 100 Mile House high schools.

She first puzzled and then astounded Chilcotin people while at the Church Ranch when she took it into her head to walk to the headwaters of Big Creek at Lorna Lake and then walk back through Empire Valley and the Gang. She took a pack horse, not to ride but to pack her tent, sleeping bag and food. She had a Samoyed dog for company. She always has a dog and has been known to pack a puppy on her backpack when hiking.

On the Big Creek trek, where there are no roads and few trails, she walked for three and a half weeks.

She got lost on the third day and before she got her bearings her tent and sleeping bag had been scraped off the pack horse. For the next three weeks she slept on the ground beside a fire as long as she was, lying on the saddle blanket. She hit one August snowstorm.

Janet walked completely through her boots. When Joe Rosette encountered her out in the Great Nowhere, a lone woman and a dog, on foot, he covered his astonishment by offering to give her boots. She had walked through her own.

Dorseys at Sky Ranch reported her lost at the 15 day mark, as they had warned her, but she got word out that she was fine and having a wonderful walk.

Many Chilcotin people have made such long trips but they were riding saddle horses and they took a few days, not a month. Only people who know that country can understand the stamina and the self-reliance that Janet required.

She has made many such trips in other parts of the plateau. She walks, on average, at least 30 miles a week, winter and summer, seldom for distances of less than 10 miles except when visiting Vancouver when she confines herself to walking the Sea Wall completely around Stanley Park once a day.

"I walked about 15 miles yesterday up Fox Mountain way and saw three big buck deer," she said, "You see so much when you walk."

She has always walked. She was one of five children whose mother raised them on a Second World War soldier's send-home pay. The only transport they could afford was their feet. To this day she still doesn't know how to ride a bicycle.

"When I was four years old I used to walk from Northfield on the edge of Nanaimo to visit my grandmother in East Wellington, about five miles each way."

Her Samoyeds died long ago of old age. She walks with two Border Collies now.

She never carries a gun and is not afraid of bears, much. She has encountered some. "I've been a bit, well, you know, a couple of times when I've come on one unexpectedly." The last time she looked the bear straight in the eye, which is exactly what you are supposed to not do, and said "You'd better move now. Just think if I was carrying a gun." The bear walked away.

She says she plans to keep on long distance walking into her eighties. Everybody west of the Fraser River believes her.

Mickey's Cougar

ANAHIM LAKE—The sad and brave death of a Princeton woman who died defending her children from a cougar reminded a few of us that heroism is all around, but only seldom is it publicly visible, and all too soon it gets forgotten. So we don't forget too much too easily, here is the story of Mickey's cougar. As far as I know it has never been told in print before, but even though it happened 70 years ago, it still deserves telling.

Her name was Hannah Tuck, daughter of a Nova Scotia ship builder who moved to the Bella Coola valley early in this century. Mickey was her nickname and it suited her well.

She grew up to be a school teacher. School teacher, telephone switchboard operator, secretary and nurse were about the only jobs available to women in those days. Today she'd have headed an air line or become a sea captain because she was able, intelligent, active, curious and boundlessly enthusiastic about almost everything she did.

As it turned out, love reared its awesome head and she married a handsome, witty, adventurous cowboy named Lester Dorsey, a man of whom it was said that after making him they broke the mould. Nobody ever accused Lester of wanting wealth or comfort.

Mickey started housekeeping in a sod roof cabin, trying to

51

cook on a flimsy sheepherder's folding tin stove. When she, Lester and Pan Phillips went into the Ulgatcho Mountains once on a pack trip and Pan proudly unpacked the wretched tin stove for her she broke into tears at seeing it again. She was as human as everybody else, just moreso.

Everybody in Chilcotin Country knew Lester and Mickey. Not all of them knew how tough a life Mickey lived, raising five children in log cabins in the back of beyond, the only place lonely enough to suit Lester who, whenever a public road reached his ranch, retreated further into the wilderness and started a new one. He was a gregarious soul but couldn't stand neighbours.

Mickey taught her children in her own kitchen where they all grew up with neither electricity, telephone nor running water. To Mickey, the hard work and danger of the frontier were just the salt and pepper which made life tasty.

She met the cougar before meeting her husband. She was 19 years old, teaching a dozen ranch kids in a one-room school house near Soda Creek on the banks of the Fraser River south of Quesnel. The kids, all young and small, had a pet goat.

One recess a child came clamouring into the schoolroom shouting that a cougar was going to eat the goat and Mickey should stop it.

Years later she talked about it. "When I went out the goat was tethered as usual to a tree, the kids were all around it, and there was a cougar which looked ready to spring.

"The only thing I could think to do was to get between the cougar and the kids. If I called them away the cat was probably going to spring at them instead of the goat."

She stood between the cougar and the kids, as she said afterward, for about one thousand years.

"I told the kids over my shoulder to go back to the nearest ranch house and get somebody. They wouldn't go. They said I'd let the cougar eat their goat. I promised and promised them I wouldn't, so eventually they went away."

She continued standing there, believing that staring down the cougar was the safest thing to do. Experts in recent years say that making eye contact with a cougar or a bear is the worst thing to do because a stare implies a threat and invites an attack. However, experts then, as now, were scarce in this country.

She remembered the cougar's stare above all else, the yellow eyes fixed on her which never seemed to blink. That and the twitch at the tip of the tail.

She was still standing, facing the cat, when somebody from the ranch house came, twenty minutes later, and shot it dead.

"When it was dead it seemed like such a poor, scrawny thing that I was ashamed of myself for being afraid," said Mickey, who did not cry, nor have hysterics nor call in psychiatrists to give trauma counselling to her and the kids. She just went back to teaching school. There was no school holiday that day.

Mickey is long dead, drowned in a plane accident at Port Hardy. Lester is dead too. They lie side by side in the tiny Anahim Lake cemetery. Their youngest, Wanda Williams, still runs the last of Lester's many ranches. Stories such as this about pioneer life are fading from memory, but they shouldn't.

The Education of Fly

HANCEVILLE—The instructions are to treat her like a Jehovah's Witness at the door of a Sunday morning. No need to get violent, but be hostile. "If you have to, throw rocks at her and miss."

This isn't all that easy if you like border collies, but there was no arguing about it. The next four days were to be the start of her formal education in herding cows, and all her attention as well as her affection had to be focussed on the cowboy who owned her.

So, although she was only seven months old and by nature friendly and playful in the way of adolescents, the little dog named Fly learned, from a few rebuffs, that she did not have another friend up on Fire Creek summer range.

From the first day she had eyes for no one except her master. By the fourth day she was developing also an eye for the cattle to be herded, which is quite a short time even for a breed as bright as the border collie.

In the educational process we were to observe, cowboy and cow dog start with one main advantage. Both have the identical instinct to make cattle move from where they are to some other place where they had not, of their own accord, thought of going.

It is an advantage that this shaggy little twelve-kilo dog, whose ancestors came from Scotland, shares with the Scots a passion for education. It likes to learn.

There are disadvantages also. Despite what the anthropomorphists suggest, dogs do not understand English or any other language. A dog cannot read words or understand a diagram. Whether it has the capacity to reason is debatable.

Fly's first lesson is to push cows that are drifting left of the line of drive back where they should be, in front of the horsemen. This cowboy's command to go left is "Way Out."

On the first day, the cowboy rides left herself as she gives the command. The dog, which had already learned to follow the human, follows this command. Soon the dog's mind takes the extra step; it runs out left on the command "Way Out" without the owner leading or following.

From this beginning, other commands are jointed on, like sections of a fishing pole, the dog's mind absorbing one section at a time.

One thing that's necessary is to train her to turn the furthest cow back into the line of drive. Her natural inclination is to turn back the first cow she reaches but, by doing so, she will often drive two or more even more distant cows further into the jack pines.

This is accomplished fairly easily by the owner repeating "Way Back" as she comes to the first stray, "Way Back" again at the second, and finally, with a subtle change of inflection, the command "Bring Her Back" at the furthest animal.

Fly gets hung up on the command for retrieving strays from the right side of the line.

The cowboy begins using the command "Come By." When she does, Fly stops, peers at her, even cocks her head to one side in puzzlement, like the old advertisement of a fox terrier listening to His Master's Voice on the gramophone.

The answer, it seems, is that "Come By" is too much the same as the command she used to summon the dog, "Come." So "Come By" is discarded and "Over" used instead.

Again, there having been a change in a command, the little dog is puzzled, but she hesitates only twice. Thereafter she knows "Over" as the order to go right.

How some other commands are transmitted remains puzzling to an observer. When Fly starts to move a cow and is stopped by the order "Leave Her Alone," how is it that she first understands what that means?

Probably it is tone of voice. Something reminds her of negative orders back at the ranch when she was younger. But it is a strange process, this communication between human and dog, and one is powerfully tempted to believe in telepathy.

Or does it all come under the word intelligence?

Wise men don't take intelligence tests among humans too seriously and testing intelligence among the other animals is an even more dubious exercise. However, like gossip, we all take part at one time or another.

Those who engage in such exercise rank the terriers and other vermin killers low on an intelligence scale, since they do no more than run out for prey and kill it. Hunting breeds are higher, the retrievers who run out to bring game back alive or dead to the handler and, above the retrievers, the pointers who direct the hunter to the game while keeping the birds still for his approach. Highest of all in this rating system are border collies and other sheep and cattle dogs who herd other animals.

True?

Who knows? Not thee, brother, nor me.

What can be said of this trip is that by the end of only three days of roundup, Fly has learned an astonishing amount. She shows a clear understanding of the riders' purpose, which is to move cows and bulls in a line ahead without losing any to right or left; also to move them slowly, so that they do not burn off their fat, but not as slowly as the ponderous old bulls would prefer.

To hurry any animal, or to move a stubborn one, Fly has learned the command "Bite 'im." To avoid getting kicked, she should nip the animal just above the hoof. Fly, however, nips higher on the hock and must someday learn, perhaps the hard way, that this is not the place to bite 'im.

Fly also needs courage.

Sooner or later a cow or bull will turn and defy her nipping. Then this mite of a dog must have the courage to throw herself at the face of this monstrously large animal and if necessary nip it on the nose to turn it. However, on this roundup, that test does not present itself to her.

When four days of riding end, Fly has left her childhood and adolescence. She is more reserved, more confident, and much, much more knowledgeable. She has even begun to develop what is called "eye."

Eye is a communication, not between dog and master, but between dog and cow, a look which conveys to the beef animal that she should abandon her thought of thrashing away into the timber because the dog has anticipated the thought.

Not once in four days does the master find it necessary to strike the dog. Only rarely is Fly scolded.

Finally it is worth noting that Fly was a happy dog.

Dogs are not happiest when sleeping in the sun with full bellies. They are happiest when doing the work they were intended to do. The same goes for humans, and for cowboys who are, as is well known, part human.

Namko's Coolee Chilco

If sorrow burdens you, pass this column by, but, stranger, as you pass, bend your knee to my dead dog because, as he died, so must you and I and every other living creature.

It's hard to know what public face to put on a death in the family. Perhaps the old British tradition of a stiff upper lip is best. But it seems better to talk about it instead. We may talk ourselves out of tears, out of the sudden loneliness which has taken the glow out of a warm orange Indian summer.

His full name was Namko's Coolee Chilco, Chinook jargon for Running Chilco of Namko. He was a Chesapeake Bay Retriever and pick of a litter of five. He had been easy to pick, more robust than the other pups, more active, but, above all, more curious about everything. Throughout his life, which was long, his face was his character, somewhat quizzical, always alert and eager.

He had all the Chesapeake failings, also, being stubborn, independent-minded and sometimes quarrelsome.

One day when he was a mature dog and fully trained, I was walking him for exercise when a man with an Airdale approached. He was a pleasant fellow, as was his dog, and he said, "Sir, I've been watching you and I want to tell you that I have never seen a dog under such perfect control as yours."

Chilco, who had dropped to sitting position at my left knee when I stopped, as he should, must have found the stranger's remarks condescending. From a sitting position he launched himself at that innocent and inoffensive Airdale and we had the damndest fight on our hands.

He was about 30 kilos, on the small side for the breed, but he was solid. When occasionally in hunting camps we cast our bones on the cold ground after a long, hard day, he would tuck himself into the small of my back at the side of the Yukon sleeping bag and we helped warm each other all night.

His nose was not as good as other dogs I have owned, but his enthusiasm compensated. He knew the bird was there and he was going to get it, no matter how long it took.

One long autumn, working by times in bramble and cactus and at others in swamp mud so thick he could not swim nor walk but had to lunge through the stuff, I shot for a whole season and never lost a single bird I saw come to the ground.

Retrievers don't last as long as other dogs. They break ice in too many duck ponds and develop arthritis. Their eyes grow cloudy. They get deaf, partly from too many muzzle blasts of the gun pounding against their ear flaps. It is always hard to tell deafness from stubbornness in a Chesapeake, but genuine loss of hearing does occur.

This fall, when he was 11, I judged he was not ready for full retirement and took him hunting again. This year our hunting was different. Chilco did not range out in grouse cover but walked at heel. It was his privilege to go to retrieve downed birds or to decline to as he chose. He always went out and brought them back proudly.

Surprising, I said to myself, how he has perked up.

Then came a two day rest at home. When we started north again, he got into the car fairly nimbly, but after seven hours riding, he could scarcely get out. His face was thin and pinched.

He was puzzled that one of his legs didn't work any more.

The Williams Lake vet took X rays which showed that a chip of his arthritic hip bone had floated into the socket. He gave him pain killers but said, "Don't fool yourself if he starts prancing around like a puppy again. He will never hunt again."

He didn't prance and the next morning I left him in camp, sleeping. We were a couple of kilometres down the road when I turned the car around. I could feel him following.

Near camp, on the little two-track trail where the poplar leaves lay in the ruts like lines of golden coins, Chilco was coming up the road on three legs. He was not going to miss hunting.

This may be my strongest memory of Namko's Coolee Chilco. Not the young, strong skookum Chilco but the old Chilco on the old narrow Chilcotin road, humping along three legged. Better to wear out than to rust out, they say.

So we put him in the back seat. We left him there when we went hunting, but when we came back with birds we handed them to him and let him hold them in his mouth and then deliver them to us in the old way. "Chilco's bird," we would say, and his tail would wag.

Last night the vet came with the merciful needle which our insane society permits for dogs but refuses to our fellow humans. Chilco's head fell in my lap in the sleep of forever and we buried him under the tree in the yard.

I don't know if talking about it is better or not. I have had to put other old companions down whom the gods decided had lived too long. You'd think it would get easier, but it never does. But thanks for listening.

A Place Lost and Lovely

BIG CREEK—Like other lovely things about the wilderness, the little lake took us by surprise.

The dog and I were following a flock of prairie chickens who had rushed off, tutting and clucking, into the pine woods.

The dog worked the crest of the hill, where the birds commonly hold after landing, and I came up at a hard trot. Of an instant, in the twinkle of an eye, as the Bible puts it, the little blue lake came into view. I could not have been more surprised to find a pearl there.

I thought I knew every lake in the Big Creek Country. I know places where lakes used to be but aren't. I have walked, run and ridden saddle horses over enough of this region to recognize almost any body of water large enough to float a Green Wing Teal. I even recognize some of the larger Douglas Firs.

I watched lakes form, grow and then go to lingering decline and death.

Abyan Meadow, which flooded and became a big lake called Happy Ann, is now a meadow again with only a couple of little potholes on it. There is no big lake, nor even a small one, at the place called Big Lake.

There are a dozen, a score and more other lakes in the Big Creek area which I have watched grow and die over the decades. The climatic cycle of this region is little understood, even though weather records have been kept since the time of the First World War. We only know that there are long periods of drought and warmth and equally long eras of wet summers and bitterly cold winters when half the land's creatures die.

Yet here, on a quiet Indian Summer afternoon, was a lake I had never seen before. Robinson Crusoe was no more surprised to find that footprint in the sand.

It was blue, clear and utterly alone, unmarked by so much as a horse trail. Tall green water reeds had grown at one end. There was a bank beaver house on a little peninsula. Unlike the temporary lakes which appear during rainy years, this one had no line of drowned timber along its shores.

This lake had been here half a century or so. Perhaps since Charlemagne's time, who can say?

I told the German Shorthair to forget about chickens and we walked quietly, respectfully, down the hill through the pines over the springy kinnikinnick bush.

Seven mallards came out, also two Barrow's Goldeneye and a pair of little Bufflehead ducks which we call Butterballs because they are so fat. I waved them away. The mallards went squawking in protest. The Goldeneyes circled us once and then came back to rest on the same water they had left. The Butterballs, being as innocent of fear as two-year-olds in a Ronald McDonald playpen, bobbed up and down in the water as if made of cork.

Two Sandhill Cranes talked foolery at the far end of the lake. A Belted Kingfisher flew off a nearby poplar and let loose his ratchet cry.

The lake, as we paced it off, was almost a kilometre long and about half as wide. A watercourse ran out of one end, dry now in the end of a long dry period which began here in early July. There was no incoming stream; the lake was fed by springs.

In the old days, when Canada was still a free country, I could have carved a notch from one of those poplars and put my mark on it, paid for a survey, paid a few dollars for a few acres and claimed it for my own. In the glorious new age, I have no such rights and bureaucrats have effective ownership of this little lake. I may enjoy it, if at all, only at their pleasure and under conditions they set. It is only a matter of a few more years and laws before I will be forbidden to sit here, flipping pebbles into the water, unless I come equipped with the necessary government permit, bearing my government social insurance number and my thumbprint.

For a few lovely minutes this day, the terrible new tyranny under which we live no longer matters. Cariboo Regional District and all its mandarins and court functionaries seem distant as people on the moon.

So for an hour or two, the German Shorthair and I can sit alone by a nameless lake, unknown to the rest of the busy world, restoring the soul.

The View from the Wineglass

RISKE CREEK—At the Wineglass Ranch, which has been run by the same family for 106 years, the ranch house is 10.5 kilometres from the front gate. The narrow trail switchbacks down 1000 metres on the breaks and banks of the Chilcotin River valley, ending in a little Eden of green grass, cottonwoods, a garden with strawberry plants and the big river which is the colour of a robin's egg. Here live the third and fourth generations of Durrells. Brian Durrell, who is the present owner-manager, says he hopes there will be Durrells running the Wineglass at the end of yet another century.

All this is very pretty and cosy, but why are we here? Just to admire the river and listen to their pen-raised pheasants screeking?

No. We are here to ask the Durrells about the future of Quebec and the rest of Canada.

Most of the metropolitan press have their own kennelbred pundits who explain Quebec to us, a stable of university political science professors who will say the kind of things the editors want to hear about Quebec, abortion, proportional parliamentary representation and the spread of the codling moth on Vancouver Island. They are all experts and if you like experts, you should be reading the paper and listening to CBC and trying to not fall off your perch with boredom.

Perhaps, over the years, you have experienced some disenchantment with experts. John F. Kennedy did, saying, after the Cuban fiasco, "All my life I have known better than to trust experts. How could I have been so stupid, to let them go ahead?"

So instead of an expert we turn to a Chilcotin rancher. He has made no studies, written no paper and he has no degrees, but he did, being more practical than theoretical in nature, hire a Quebec teenager for a cowboy one summer a few years ago. "Best worker I ever had. Worked hard. Enthusiastic. Loved this country."

When the boy went home at the end of the summer he invited the Durrells to come and visit him and his family at Ste. Agathe. They went, Brian, his wife, Janet, in the final stages of her third pregnancy, and two children. They had a great time, canoed on wild rivers in La Belle Province, met many of the French Canadians who call themselves the "pure wool" French, which means no admixture of the English in the family.

In the quiet way ranchers have, they watched. Janet noticed that the children in Ste. Agathe seemed never to cry, and when she came back to B.C., hearing children cry in public was unsettling. They both noticed that their cowboy's family, overwhelmingly friendly though they might be, were clearly fearful that their son might leave Quebec for The West, and clearly The West was not where they wanted him or any of their children to be as permanent residents.

Since the Durrells came home, the families continue to correspond. They become closer, year by year. The Durrells are considering sending their children to Quebec for a year's schooling in French.

This is to give a thumbnail sketch as background to the one big question, will Quebec remain part of Canada?

"No," says Brian, "I think they will leave. They'll form a separate country, and so will we. But I also think that, years down the line, they'll be reunited with the rest of Canada. Leave, and then rejoin, that's what my instinct tells me."

"After all," says Janet, "it's the same as the Indians here in Chilcotin. We've tried to get along and it hasn't worked all that well. There are people who are different and want to be different."

We talked until the pool of night had filled the valley of the Chilcotin with darkness and spilled over the last traces of sunset on the hills above. As we did, it became apparent how the view of these people was different from that of the chattering classes.

Brian and Janet didn't talk about the machinery of separation or the constitutional labyrinth through which we might have to pick our way. As for politics, neither of them mentioned, even once, the politicians of the Quebec or federal parties.

They dealt instead with the things unseen but strongly felt, the spirit that moves one group of people or another, of impulses which may have no easy relationships with rationality. Out of this, far more than from logical thought, come our collective and our individual choices in life, to be continentalists, to be isolated, to be ranchers or poets or soldiers or, for that matter, to be political scientists. Quebec, as they see it, is all a matter of feeling.

How Red Lost His Ranch

BIG CREEK—Last Saturday, Red Allison and other friends of the late Ronnie Tomlinson came up to Twilight Ranch and, in the grove of golden poplar where Ronnie's ashes are scattered, they erected a small plaque in his memory.

It's four years since the guy died, which proves that people up here still haven't got a very good handle on that thing called time, but the thought was good.

There are a lot of thoughts about Twilight Ranch, Ronnie Tomlinson, and Red Allison: thoughts of hope, of sadness, and, in the end, with Red, something a trifle noble shining through.

My first note on Red Allison relates to a Williams Lake stampede of about twenty years ago. Red was drunker than fourteen hundred dollars and so was his companion. Fancying they had some disagreement, Red took a roundhouse swing at the chin of his buddy, missed by about a foot and a half, lost his balance, and tried to save himself from falling by grabbing his opponent's belt. The other fellow lost his balance and they both fell into the dust.

Red turned his big, pink, boyish face to the other and snarled: "Why can't you SHTAND UP and FIGHT like a MAN?" Clearly, Red was a man of some distinction, and so it proved.

Over the years he did many things, always well. For quite a few years he ran the general store at Riske Creek in Chilcotin. When the big OK Ranch on the other side of the Fraser River was in absentee ownership, Red was manager, again for many years.

He raised a family and a good reputation but made no great amount of money. He had a little piece of land here, another little piece there. He has a little piece in the Clinton area now.

Also, for a number of years, he was a silent partner in the Twilight Ranch here at Big Creek. Ronnie Tomlinson, a very quiet Englishman from Yorkshire, couldn't raise enough money for a down payment when the place came up for sale. Red came in on shares.

Ronnie proved to be an excellent rancher. The Twilight grew just a bit better, year by year. Fences were renewed. New grazing leases were acquired. Land was cleared. Always it was done a little bit at a time because that's how the money to do it came in, one dollar at a time.

At about the time the Twilight began to look like a model small ranch, Ronnie complained to his cowboy one morning that he felt funny, somehow, and was going to lie down. Twenty minutes later he was dead of a heart problem that he never knew he had.

Since he was a bachelor and clearly had had no thoughts about dying in middle age, people were not surprised when no will was found. So in the normal process of law, the Twilight was sold, Red was paid off for his share, and the balance, a sizable bite out of a million-dollar bill, went to Ronnie's old mother in England.

Red would have dearly loved to have taken over Twilight. It was a ranch just of a size and type for him and his family to run. But a couple of things had happened since he first became a silent partner. Ronnie had repaid Red a fair portion of what he contributed. More, Ronnie had so improved the place, and speculators had driven all ranch prices so high, that it was impossible for

Red to raise enough cash to buy Ronnie's share of the place from the estate.

Last fall, three years after Ronnie's death, I ran into Red at a Williams Lake cattle auction where he was buying, selling, and just poking around. It was a shame, I said, that he did not become the owner of the Twilight place, there in the shallow valley of the Bambrick Creek with the green pine hills standing over the yellow grass meadows.

"Oh, then you don't know the rest of the story," he said. He giggled. He is a big man, over six feet, and mostly made of muscle, but he has always had a high-pitched girlish voice and a girlish giggle. He must have had a hard time with both during school days.

No, I knew no more to the story.

Well, Red said, not long ago he got a call from a Williams Lake lawyer. This lawyer had taken over the files of another Williams Lake lawyer who had died, or gone to Heaven, Hell, or the Supreme Court, wherever it is lawyers go when they quit working.

"He had only just got around to going through these cardboard boxes full of the other lawyer's files and what does he find but Ronnie Tomlinson's will. There it is, all signed, sealed, and proper, and it leaves the entire ranch to me."

"What are you going to do, Red?"

"Well, the lawyer said a will is a will and this is a real one. If I went to court, I could overturn everything that had happened and get the Twilight. But of course, I couldn't do that.

"Can you imagine me asking some judge to tell Ronnie's old mother in England that she has got to give all that money back to me? I couldn't possibly do a thing like that."

So he told the lawyer to forget the whole business and let the tail go with the hide. His last tie with Twilight was cut last Saturday when he put the plaque in the poplar grove so men would remember his partner.

Joe's Electric and the Truck That Drove Itself

BIG CREEK—Character shapes companies and the character of Ryan Watt shaped a company here called Joe's Electric, a company that, alas, the world has now lost.

Ryan was a ranch kid, one of a bunch raised at the Breckness ranch in Big Creek, Chilcotin. All the brothers and sisters were different one from another, as usual. Ryan's difference was that he liked to listen rather than to talk and to be unnoticed rather than noticed.

Twenty years ago that characteristic brought him to the attention of the police.

An RCMP constable on a rare visit to Big Creek passed a farm truck that was bustling along the road with nobody driving it. Being a policeman, he was naturally curious and decided to investigate the phenomenon.

When he turned round and followed the truck he thought he could see the head of a small child that barely came above the dashboard to peep through the steering wheel. It was Ryan, age eleven, who was on his way to the one-room Big Creek school.

He had bolted wood blocks to the brake and clutch pedals so his feet would reach them, and except on hard bumps when he sat low in the seat, he was always able to see over the dash to the road.

But when the constable got the truck pulled over, there was still nobody in it. Ryan had slipped out the passenger door and was crouched beside it. "I was terrified," he says now. "There were almost as many Bengal tigers in Chilcotin then as there were policemen."

When the constable came round one side of the truck, Ryan went the opposite way, always keeping the vehicle between them. "I could see which way his boots were turning, looking under the truck," he recalls.

After two full circuits of the truck the pair finally met one another and the policeman was reasonable enough. He just told Ryan not to practise driving on the public highway, and Ryan refrained from saying that was how he and his brother went to school every day.

When he became an electrician and set himself up in business in Williams Lake, Ryan clung to the view that there is no point in bringing yourself to other people's attention needlessly. When his accountant set up Ryan's company, he asked what the name should be.

"Let's say it's my dog's business—call it Joe's Electric," said Ryan, pointing at his Labrador retriever, which was sleeping, as usual.

At that time, as when he drove the driverless truck, he did not foresee how hard anonymity is to achieve in this world. His customers kept asking for Joe. "I would say, 'Well, it's not a good day to see Joe. He was out on the town last night and he's in pretty tough shape today. If you must talk to him, go out in the yard. He's sleeping under the truck.'

"Lots of people would ask why Ryan Watt was signing Joe's Electric cheques. I would always tell them the truth—that he was sitting out in the truck, that he wasn't working today and hadn't worked all week, or that I hadn't seen him since Tuesday."

He could also explain that Joe, although the best sort you

could ever hope to meet, the kind you'd be willing to go hunting with, did have his imperfections and that the truth of the matter was he had never learned to read and couldn't even write his own name.

There were, perhaps, those who became puzzled when they demanded and received the full name of Joe of Joe's Electric. It was Gunanoot's Joe of Terror.

In time, Joe died, as dogs do. Ryan got another dog, a springer spaniel. It was good at busting grouse out of heavy cover but, Ryan says, it didn't have the temperament for business. It lacked the solidity, the stability of the Labrador.

Joe's Electric disappeared from the Williams Lake yellow pages. Ryan now helps run a motorcycle agency with the ordinary, everyday, and uninspiring name Williams Lake Honda.

Perce's Rubber Worm

ANAHIM LAKE—Every time an election is called I think about Perce Hance and the rubber worm.

All the Hances of Hanceville were gentlemanly except for a couple of lady Hances who were ladylike. The original Chilcotin Hance, Tom, came from the American South, where manners rank higher than money on the social scale. His several sons and daughter were taught that once you abandoned good manners you had lost any argument, no matter how good your position had been to start with.

Percy, eldest of the family, first white child born west of the Fraser River, held tenaciously to that view. Perce never killed anybody or, so far as I know, ever hit anybody particularly hard. However, if Perce Hance intended to kill you, he was the kind of man who would first make a small bow and present you with an Easter lily in prime condition to hold in your left hand before he shot you.

One night at the old TH Ranch, when night's candles were burning out and the whisky running low, Marian Witte asked if anyone would care for food and Perce said well, many thanks, and might it be possible for him to have just one small sandwich.

She made him a roast beef sandwich in the kitchen. Somebody

73

I shall not identify, except to say that it was not me, went to a fishing tackle box, removed a long rubber worm, and put it in the sandwich. By the time Perce got his sandwich, several people in the room knew it had a gutta-percha lining and there was high expectancy.

Perce took a bite and became thoughtful. He bit again. He bit as hard as a man with store teeth top and bottom can bite.

There was a sound like a sharp string breaking. Perce chewed and swallowed that first bite.

It was the moment to shout "Happy April Ferce, Perce." Nobody did. He spoke first.

"Exactly what I wanted," he said. "There is nothing tastier than a good beef sandwich."

All impulses to cheers or laughter died away and were replaced by a broad dismay. Should he be warned? Was there anything poisonous about artificial fishworms, coloured purple, as sold by Army & Navy in Vancouver?

Anything that could have been said should have been said immediately, and since it was not said there remained only general apprehension.

Perce slowly, gamely, ate the whole sandwich. A bounce at a time, as someone said later.

He declined the offer of another beef sandwich. The first, he said, had been perfect. He died, many years later, without knowing about the rubber worm.

Now of course some people will say, what has this got to do with elections?

Well, it has a lot to do with elections.

After the eating of the rubber worm there was a lot of silence lying around that room, and somebody offered up a political story. It contained, he said, everything that anybody need ever know about the art of politics and it all happened one hot summer's day on Becher's Prairie, just up the road a piece.

"From Becher House they could see this truck coming across the range. It would run maybe a hundred, two hundred yards. Then it would stop. The driver would get out with a piece of two-by-four in his hand. He would slam the two-by-four on the sides of the truck box. Then he would run back to the cab and drive another hundred yards or so before he did it again.

"When he got to Becher House somebody said, 'Could you tell us exactly what is going on?'

"The driver said: 'Yes. It's very simple. This is a one-ton truck. I am packing two tons of canaries in it. I have got to keep at least half of them flying all the time.'"

Now you, too, understand all about politics. Keep at least half of the people up in the air all the time. And you understand why every time an election writ drops I think about Perce Hance and a rubber worm.

Kitchen Midden

My heart is in Chilcotin but I left my
liver at the Lakeview Hotel.
—Old Cariboo saying, author unknown

WILLIAMS LAKE—Archaeologists dig up what are called kitchen middens to discover the shape of life in societies of long ago. They find broken household implements, knives, beads, and all the bits and pieces that formed a community's life.

It is in this sense that Randy Brunner's collection of notes from the night clerks of the Lakeview Hotel should be viewed. The notes are a discovery, one that our province may well wish to preserve, as we preserve old Indian middens. But for the treasure you must sift tons of waste.

Randy, who died in 1981, was owner and manager of the Lakeview from 1950 to 1975. The old hotel is itself a monument. It was built in the 1890s and was extended a couple of times since. It is now being renovated again. At the time these notes were entered it was the old, familiar, rambling place, a bit cluttered, often infested with mice and sometimes cockroaches. It was and is a watering hole for ranchers, cowboys, and Indians out of Chilcotin and other parts of the Back of Beyond.

The night clerks' notes were made on spiral stenographer's notepads. The handwriting of several staff people is to be found. Randy and his clerks made the notebooks a central information depot. Therein they exchanged jokes, gossip, and the tedious details of broken Coke machines, missing linens, and that ever-present phenomenon of hotel operation, the india-rubber cheque.

"When M. comes in ask if he needs a room for Stampede as he is a Regular." Another staffer writes: "A regular something, alright."

"Anita. Young punks were very good Friday so guess they had to make up for it Saturday. Foam pillows in 104 and 105 need recovering."

"If Polly B. is out of her suite don't let her son have the key. He has too many friends."

"Just read your note about Duane W. not having any water in his room. After 48 hours at Guides' Convention guess he had a fire to put out."

"Aussie hears there is a girl serving drinks at the Chilcotin Inn. What will they do next there?" (This, a notation from the year 1968, not 1908. How fast some of our ideas changed!)

The Pacific Great Eastern morning train couldn't leave the station because the crew at the Lakeview didn't get wake-up calls.

The café refused to give a second cup of coffee free to a regular guest. He knows Randy will want to know of this atrocity. John W. in 204 is more plaintive than bellicose ... "doesn't mind mice in the room but objects when they crawl into bed with him."

"114 took his 'wife' up. I peeled the bark off him. He said 'We've been married for 17 years.' I said 'Congratulations, now get her the hell out of here.'" (Two days later, 114 thanks the clerk for his discriminating kindness and this too goes into the record.)

"Watch 218. Heavy drinker AND smoker."

Alcohol runs all through the narrative. Often it's funny but the sad and the sordid aspects of the drug are there too. "T. in 221 has not come in yet. Little girl still there. Suggest you check for her breakfast, etc."

The next note, in other handwriting: "Girls are looking after T's daughter but if he asks DON'T tell him what room they're in as he is gassed."

A day later: "T. rather pugnacious [sic] at desk so told him what I thought of his neglect of child. Reminded him of his debt to office staff for feeding the child, etc."

There are guests who are loved. Money is loaned to them, errands are run, phone calls made, wives pacified. There are others whose arrival is regarded much as Vienna anticipated the arrival of the Turkish army.

One such is John P. of Chilcotin who throws his empty bottles out the window and narrowly misses pedestrians. He can't be broken of the habit but he must be taken in because his category is a Regular. A Regular is something like a king or a pope. You can't just boot his ass out onto the street.

There is an exchange of notes as to whether a change of the moon is the main factor influencing the behaviour of hotel guests.

The vast, the overwhelming bulk of the notes in the spiral-lock pads are, like fragments in a kitchen midden, the multitudinous chores of housekeeping, the ceaseless lament of a mother picking up after the members of a vast, careless, irresponsible, charming, and occasionally impossible family. Ironing, burned-out lights, torn linen, and bathrooms that didn't get cleaned; messages, money for safekeeping, slow pays, plugged toilets, worn carpets, noise, underage girls, lost keys, the heat, the cold, the drafts, and windows that won't open.

"211 tried to talk me into thinking the Communist government in U.S.S.R. is better than our capitalist gov. Why don't people who think Russia is so good go there?" (Other handwriting) "They're too lazy, Russians are too smart to let them in."

Set beside Randy Brunner's twenty kilos of notebooks, can the records of the Pearson, Trudeau, or Clark cabinet meetings serve as well to document the realities of our age? Not as far as Williams Lake is concerned they can't.

The Cariboo Alligator

WILLIAMS LAKE—While scratching an irritating itch of the mind with the thin toothpick of memory, I find I have dislodged a morsel of Cariboo history that is almost forgotten.

Almost forgotten, but not entirely forgotten. Dozens, scores of men attending this year's Williams Lake Stampede will, I am sure, recall these events. They are a portion of history which is not really lost. Rather, they have been mislaid. Men have failed to note their passing, failed to note that they have slipped imperceptibly out of the present and into the forever-frozen area of human affairs which we call the past.

The events I would like to resurrect here—and I trust some eye will distill a tear for their memory during stampede—are the great annual alligator migrations which were so striking a feature of life in the Cariboo country a few years ago.

The alligators were shy creatures—modest, unassuming, and unspectacular except during the fall migrations. Their northerly drift in spring out of the Okanagan was seldom noticed. They had, as a rule, paired up before crossing the Coldstream Ranch at Vernon. They moved furtively and usually by night. Not surprisingly, the pairs were interested only in one another as they made their way north to the nesting grounds.

Their favourite grounds were Miocene, Puntzi, and Anahim Lake. There were also small summer colonies at Nmiah Valley, Spain Lake, and Australian Bar. No doubt there were scores of other regions which they inhabited during the summer season, but no reliable records were kept in those districts. The country was large and the Northwest Alligator (*Alligator caigator impulsivus*) was a small species. The immensity of the land swallowed them up.

Occasionally the roaring of the bulls might be heard on a June night, as they fought for the privilege of associating with their neighbour's wives. But these were the only sounds. The females were silent. An admirable quality, since lost to the country. Females laid, according to status, 29 to 68 soft-shell eggs in mounds of rotting vegetation. The young hatched, usually, just before the Anahim Lake Stampede. They were not trapped. The pelts were poor during breeding season. Occasionally, their omnivorous appetites would lead them to devour a stray dog or an extra child. But they posed no threat to stock, and cattlemen therefore considered them harmless.

Alligator impulsivus was accepted as being just another variety of Cariboo fauna, no more surprising in its presence than the white pelican or the eastern brook trout. They were not popular. But neither were they feared or disliked. In terms of general interest, they ranked ahead of provincial secretaries, but behind university presidents.

Only in autumn, during the great migrations, did they attract any general notice. This migration preceded that of the sandhill cranes, but was usually a week to ten days later than that of the white pelicans. It was led by the bulls, followed by the cows. The young, those which had not already been eaten by their parents (*Alligator impulsivus* was a notoriously sloppy feeder) came last.

The young were, by this time, little more than fourteen to sixteen inches in length. But they were robust, their lavender-tinted bellies swelled with the ripgut hay on which they had been obliged to subsist for the first weeks after hatching.

The movement was generally confined to the creeks. But the general flow of the creeks in Cariboo is westward—an error of Providence which has not yet been rectified. The alligator swarms were bound south to the Columbia River, not west to the Pacific Ocean. As a result, the streams of the migration were obliged to travel overland frequently. Short in the leg but heavy in the claw, these columns of migrating reptiles scoured rocky trails across the grasslands and through the jack pines. These trails were deep, rough, and narrow.

Many of the old alligator tracks can still be found. The Chilcotin Road, for instance, was originally an alligator track. Many sections of it remain unchanged to this day. The Chilcotin strain made its crossing of the Fraser just below Christine's Cabin at the edge of the original Home Valley of the Gang.

At the confluence of the Chilcotin and Fraser rivers, they would meet the contingents out of Australian and Miocene and there would be a brief but colourful frolic.

The migrants then moved overland through the Place Ranch at Dog Creek, travelling, usually, between the hours of 3:00 and 4:00 A.M. The roaring of the bulls, the harsh clatter of curved claws on the gravel, and the thump of heavy tails on the sod— all these sounds made a clamour in the night. But the residents paid little heed. "It is just the alligator migration going through," men would say, any who chanced to be awake in those small hours.

Suddenly the migrations dwindled. A few people began to comment that there weren't as many alligators as in the old days, but such comments drew little attention. By the time it was apparent that the population was facing extinction, the trend had become irreversible.

The provincial game department did everything in its power to preserve the species by opening a hunting season on cows and calves, but they were apparently too late in taking these heroic measures. The race was doomed.

Why, we do not know. Perhaps it was a change of climate or of vegetation, perhaps new diseases and predators. Perhaps it was simply the advance of Hydro, blacktop, loan sharks, and other appurtenances of civilization. Probably it was a combination of all these factors which combined to extinguish the race, thus repeating the tragedy of the dinosaur colony at Miocene.

In 1958, Martin von Riedemann of the Alkali Lake Ranch trapped one of the last alligators seen in the Cariboo country. It was a small, undernourished male (otherwise he would never have roped it).

The country owes an unacknowledged debt to Mr. Riedemann. He worked hard on that alligator's behalf. He nursed the animal back to health. Its colour improved. It developed into a Bay, with three white stockings. The Riedemanns built a pool for it beside the home place and hand-fed it. It liked Wienerschnitzel.

In June, 1961, Mr. Riedemann imported a female Florida alligator (*Alligator missississipiensis*) and put it into the pool with the male.

"We just hoped that when they saw one another, they would think of something to do," said Mr. Riedemann.

But the experiment was unsuccessful. The male, which had always had a sultry temperament, went cultus. In August of that year, he accompanied some of the cowboys on a party in Williams Lake, checked out of the Lakeview Hotel on the second morning and has never been seen since.

The female remained in the creek until November, 1963, when her life was cut short by a Vancouver hunter who shot her, mistaking her for a mule. As far as is known, she was the last alligator in the Cariboo country.

How little trace of the species remains! There is one faded photograph of one of the Mulvahill boys riding one—they had thrown a saddle on it, for a joke. But that is all.

Let us weep for them. We shall not see their like again.

A Judicial View of
the Cariboo Alligator

MONTREAL—A couple of months ago, when I was in British Columbia, I wrote a column about the great Cariboo alligator migrations. My mail having finally caught up with me at this drop, I find myself indebted to Chief Justice J. O. Wilson of the B.C. Supreme Court for further information on this now-extinct species. Mr. Justice Wilson's letter is as follows:

I am glad that you have recorded some of the facts about *Alligator caigator impulsivus*. Well do I remember the spring night when a couple of them chewed the tires off my Winton Six in front of the 141 Mile House.

You will recall that Schulmann, in his otherwise impeccable treatise, stated that these saurians were indigenous to the Columbia Basin and indeed presumed to name them *Alligator schulmanni columbiensis*. Some state documents recently found under a bed in the Escorial prove him wrong.

In 1584, Jan Vanderploenck, a Dutch navigator in the service of the Viceroy of Spain, found the mouth of the Columbia and ascended the river as far as the

Cascades. When he returned to Acapulco, he gave, in his halting Spanish, a glowing account of the new country, stressing its fruitfulness. The Viceroy said: 'Wonderful, Captain, and since it is a fruitful country, you must, when you return there, stock it with my favourite alligator pears.'

Vanderploenck, whose knowledge of Spanish was rudimentary, made the very natural mistake of thinking that His Excellency wanted the land stocked with pairs of alligators. He shipped a deckload of these at the mouth of the Orinoco and took them to the Cascades, where he turned them loose. They bred, portaged the various falls of the Columbia, and eventually made their way into the Okanagan and the Cariboo. Governor Simpson tried unsuccessfully, in the 1840s, to put them down because of their propensity for kit beavers.

Vanderploenck, ironically, was himself consumed by alligators when he fell off a raft on the Amazon in 1596.

In response to this letter, I can only say that the information it contains surprises me. Because the name of the Asian strain, *caigator,* appears in the Latin name of the Columbia alligator, I had jumped to the conclusion that there had been an infusion of Oriental blood into the West Coast reptiles, possibly as a result of some strays being swept off the China coast by the Japanese Current. (There is no doubt that those which once populated the Cariboo had slanted eyes. Numerous observers have recorded this feature.) But I am not prepared to dispute with a man whose research has carried him to Acapulco and Madrid.

I would like to note, however, that all too few students of West Coast history take the pains to put their findings on paper before the last strands of history's hawser are snapped by the pull of time. There must be many British Columbians who remember the great alligator migrations of the Cariboo. Will they speak now? Or will they take their memories, together with the old-age pension and some Dow Brewery stock, to Cuernevaca or Maui or some other place where the value of their information is not appreciated?

The Sidehill Gouger Situation

VANCOUVER—We have some new and exciting information today about two little-known B.C. wildlife species, the Cariboo alligator and the sidehill gouger. For this, we are in the debt of two men who make an avocation of natural history. They have gone out in the field, where earnest researchers should be, and they have used their powers of observation well. They have been active while too many of the rest of us, I fear, have been sitting around in PTA committee meetings, raking leaves, chopping firewood, and engaging in other vulgar and futile pursuits. Our first report is from Norman Shaw of Powell River:

> Some time ago, in one of your columns in *The Sun,* I noted a reference to that curious and engaging animal, the sidehill gouger (*Lopsidium sardonicus*). May I offer the following observations which were made in the Ashnola district of the Similkameen country.
>
> Sidehill gougers were once plentiful on those hills, although I fear they are now nearing extinction. A great loss to all lovers of nature. Originally, all the gougers of this area were of the right-hand variety. That is, both of the right legs were longer than the left,

and they were therefore compelled to graze the mountains in a counterclockwise direction. In the early twenties, however, a number of left-hand sidehill gougers appeared.

When two of the same sex but of opposite type met on a mountainside a fierce battle would ensue. The loser, in the agony of defeat, would momentarily forget its natural limitations, turn tail to flee and inevitably fall to its death. If the meeting were between opposite sexes, the result was equally unfortunate, although more interesting. The animals would attempt to mate, but would almost always die of frustration and exhaustion.

Occasionally, by the exercise of the utmost perseverance and ingenuity, equalled in the animal kingdom only by the porcupine, a union would be consummated. The offspring were uniformly unfortunate.

The hybrids were of three types. One was the *high-behinded* sidehill gouger. It could only travel uphill and invariably died of starvation on the top of the mountain on which it was born. All the higher peaks of the Ashnola contain a few pitiful heaps of their bones. The *low-behinded* sidehill gouger was once considered a separate species (*Lopsidium sauras*). Its fate was similar to that of the high-behinded variety. As for the third type, *corner-high*, these unfortunates couldn't move anywhere. The devoted parents would attempt to bring food to the young, but since they had to make a complete circuit of the mountain for every feeding, starvation naturally ensued.

We can only be grateful that at least in the remote vastness of the Cariboo country, the haunting calls of the gougers may still be heard. For how long, one wonders.

One does wonder. But, on to more cheerful information. There is evidence that the Cariboo alligator (*Alligator caigator impulsivus*) has not only retained some territory in the Cariboo, but has also spread to the western coast of Vancouver Island. The report is from Jules Cariou of Port Alice on the west coast of Vancouver Island. He writes:

> Am shipping by separate container a specimen of your famous Cariboo alligator, found by myself in the Rumble Beach area. This specimen was bagged November 2 in the morning, before the sun had crossed the yardarm.
>
> I was hunting by myself, with a 300 Savage, when I came upon the alligator near a washed-out bridge—the only kind of bridge we have in this country. The creature was unmistakable. The colouring was right—dark scaly top-hide, golden red belly, beady black eyes, and long in the tooth and claw. I did not shoot him. He was dying when I found him.
>
> I laid the 300 Savage on the ground and walked up beside him. Then I sat down to think about it. I lit my pipe and smoked it upside down (so I wouldn't drown) and thought a long time.
>
> I can't say that it was a very pleasant time, me gurgling on the pipe and the alligator approaching the climax of his biography with considerable rolling of the eyes. And the wind was cold and sharp as a Wilkinson blade after the thirteenth shave. I will not remember this as one of my favourite occasions.
>
> After a while, the alligator expired. I made a yoke of the 300 Savage and dragged him home. I am sure you will know where to stuff him.

The Land Where Diogenes
Put Out His Lantern

ALEXIS CREEK—A few reports from Chilcotin, the country where
Diogenes finally put out his lantern . . .

The Downwind Tracker's wife reports on winter in Big Creek:

"We set off with the milk cow to take her to the bull to be bred.
The Downwind Tracker was on the tractor. He likes to be driver.
He dragged the wagon which had three bound bales of hay and
me on it. At the end of a long rope was the Jersey.

"She came along all right at first but about halfway there she
remembered how much trouble she'd got into with bulls before
and started slewing around. We had a long march.

"Five minutes after meeting the bull she decided he wasn't her
type and beat a trail for the home place with him in pursuit. I
can't blame her in a way—he is big and nasty and needlessly
masculine.

"When we returned from feeding the bull had her up against
the hay shed. The Downwind Tracker drove the tractor right in
between them and the Jersey went galloping off into three-foot
snowdrifts.

"The Downwind Tracker said, 'Catch her, catch her.' I started

plowing through the snow. My husband, still sitting on the tractor, then hollers, 'Run, before he beats you to her.'

"We didn't talk much to one another at dinnertime."

The *Globe and Mail,* which collects statistics, reports that the
number of full-time farmers in Canada has now dropped to
90,000, while the number of full-time civil servants in the various
governments' agricultural departments, which are devoted to
looking after farmers, has reached 18,000.

There is now one person writing memorandums for every five
people forking the raw manure.

The *Economist* magazine, examining Russia's agriculture,
finds that in that country's agricultural industry one person in
three is a government employee. This shows how advanced
Communists are in planning.

Given time, in both nations the number of bureaucrats will
exceed the number of farmers. There will come a day when the
entire industry is composed of bureaucrats and nobody is left to
grow spuds, raise beef, watch the northern lights at calving time
or otherwise complicate flow charts which will, by then, have
been finally perfected.

In Chilcotin when a woman has twins there are four of them.

Chilcotin has further contributed to the expansion of the English
language as follows:

Chilcotin dragline: a shovel

Chilcotin overdrive: coasting downhill in neutral

Chilcotin credit card: a gas siphon hose

Chilcotin holiday: leaving home for several days with no
more provisions than one horse, one rifle and one shaker
of salt

Chilcotin cheque: cash

Chilcotin sandwich: a shot of whisky and a dry, folded napkin,
  provided in establishments whose liquor licence forbids
  serving alcoholic beverages except with meals
Chilcotin socket wrench set: a pair of slip joint pliers
Chilcotin turkey: a river-run salmon which has been illegally
  dip-netted by a white or legally netted by an Indian and then
  illegally sold to a white; the flavour comes from the illegality

Further samples of the English language as it is booted around in
Chilcotin:
  Description of a truly rank horse: "I would know that horse
    again if I met him as hide on a pair of boots in Halifax."
  A rodeo cowboy telling how he was thrown by a great bucking
    horse: "I had never before seen the stampede grounds from
    that altitude."
  About another ornery shitter: "He was one of them horses it
    takes you a long time to get on him but scantly any time to
    get off him."

The Corporate Beef Drive

A long time ago, when I was more stupid, I learned almost every-thing about the economics of the beef industry from my friend Duane Witte. We were moving his cattle from the spring grass in the valley of the Chilcotin River to his summer range.

He ran a cow-calf outfit. Soon after our little drive, much of the beef industry shifted to farm and feedlot operations and, as we all know, ever since then things have got more and more won-derful until finally we got to where we are now. But I speak of an old-fashioned open-range operation, back in the days when earth was young—about 1975.

Down in the valley of the Chilcotin that year the whole opera-tion of moving his cattle came to depend on the health and spirit of one old grade Hereford cow. She had aborted and been discov-ered prostrated on a narrow bench, two hundred metres up from the river, five hundred metres down from the cow camp. The trail to her was about as steep as a pitched roof on a ski lodge.

Two or three times a day we would clamber down that slope on our saddle horses. We carried a pail of water, a sack of grain, and a rifle. The plan was that if she looked sicker, Duane would shoot her and we would get on with the drive. If she showed any cheerfulness we would feed her, water her, give her some Dr. Bell's and lift her to her feet for a few minutes.

Somehow, to Duane, she always looked cheerful.

To get her on her feet he and I would work the front end and his cowboy, Bobbie Brush, would crank the tail to get her hind end up. To anyone not experienced in getting a cow in this condition on her feet the advice is, never take the south end of the job. Bobbie would stand there, his Levis streaming, and from time to time he would say, plaintively, "I should have been a brain surgeon, like Mother wanted."

After three days the cow became infected with some of Duane's optimism, so the beef drive proceeded from Spring Turnout to his summer range at Teepee Heart Ranch in Big Creek. Even during the drive, Duane made two seventy-five-kilometre round trips to the Turnout to check on her condition and stopped only because she eventually walked off. It turned out later that she took up with a Gang Ranch bull on the nearby range. She had obviously forgotten what had given her all her trouble in the first place.

To get a grasp of the economics of this operation I applied to Duane's wife, Marian. Why days of delay and wear and tear on trucks and men when an eleven-cent bullet could have been used?

"No problem," she said. "It just means that when we sell her we will have to get four times as much as has ever been paid for a cow at a Williams Lake auction. That's all. Someday, if you bite into that cow at McDonald's, just remember you are eating twenty-dollar-a-pound beef."

If they ever got that price I never heard of it. My suspicion is that the sick cow was one of the reasons that Duane never drove BMWs or had movie stars for mistresses.

You may well ask what would be the use of offering advice to Duane about cash flow and such matters. He was a typical rancher and would doubtless give the classic response: "Hell, man, I don't need good advice. I am not running this outfit half as good as I already know how to."

But it may be suggested that this account of an overoptimistic rancher and his cow should not be left here. It could help our understanding of the world if we take a look at how other people might have handled the cow.

In my life I have had much contact with bureaucracies. They usually win while I lose, so they must be smarter than me.

How would a big government bureaucracy or the bureaucracy of any large private corporation handle the cow on the sidehill? Consider first how many divisions would have to be deployed.

There would be Medical (the cow was sick), Accountancy (who else to keep track of overtime?), and Public Information to keep the Greenpeace people away; also Personnel (the union shop steward would almost certainly show up), the Agricultural Department (Crown grazing land was involved), and Support Services for tents, cookhouses, first-aid stations, mobile repair shops, fax machines, and separate but equal bathroom facilities for female staff.

A task force would be formed.

There would be any God's amount of planning, something in which they say the rest of us are lamentably deficient, and no prairie blizzard could match the amount of paper filling the sky.

One great misfortune, and a very common one, might complicate matters. If it turned out that two vice-presidents or two deputy ministers had an almost equal involvement in the project, all planning, all activity would come to a halt while the two people fought out the important battle—who was to be kept off whose turf?

In the end, a turf battle is usually referred upstairs, to a capital city such as Victoria or Ottawa or, in the case of private industry, to a corporate headquarters in Toronto or New York. The mails, it will be recalled, don't move as rapidly now as in the nineteenth century and the delay is becoming as long as an arctic winter.

As any normal person can perceive, by the time the rescue convoy hits the road the cow is long dead. But some normal people still don't perceive that in a bureaucratic operation, this makes no difference whatsoever. Forms have been made and signed, flow charts have been drawn, a system and a policy have been put in place. If these function as expected, the operation will be successful and its original purpose, if the original purpose can be remembered by anyone, will be a trivial detail.

Out in the ill-organized world of ranchers, farmers, fishermen, small businessmen and the other rabble of society there are an extraordinary number of people who cannot grasp one simple truth—in a big operation it is not what you accomplish that counts but how extensively you have organized your activities.

People who don't recognize this because of purposeful obtuseness deserve all the indignities and costs which big government and big business heap upon them.

Of course, despite all the committee meetings, the great cow rescue operation would probably not proceed according to plan. As one of the B.C. government's most highly paid servants once cheerfully assured me, "Anything that can go wrong will go wrong."

If losses are under half a million dollars, they can probably be hidden under Miscellaneous in the annual report. However, at higher figures it may be necessary to form a task force or a royal commission to examine the matter and to ensure that the innocent are punished and the guilty promoted.

All things considered, I prefer Duane's way.

He lost on the cow rescue operation but it was his loss, not mine. When big business or big government loses money, I am expected to cough up money so that profits and executive salaries are safeguarded. The more the big outfits lose, the higher my taxes and the prices of everything I buy.

Also, it is worth mentioning that doing it Duane's way meant there was one more cow in the world than there would otherwise have been, and that cannot be entirely bad.

Longhorns, Again,
at the Oldest Ranch

ALKALI LAKE—Here on the oldest ranch in Canada, under a frosty late autumn sunset which is red as a russet apple, all the air of the valley is shaken by the lamentations of 330 cows who have been separated from their calves, who have just been weaned. Such loud melancholy may have attended the expulsion of the ten tribes of Israel. The calves also wail about it.

In our time there is no such mourning except that of captains of industry who find their corporations suddenly deprived of government welfare payments. Industrialists, like beef calves, lament when asked to stand on their own feet and seek their own nourishment.

Fourteen hundred calves this year, Doug Mervyn says. That is 500 more than when he bought Alkali Lake Ranch a little more than nine years ago.

Doug does not wish to be known as a gentleman rancher. He wants the place to be a model ranch, which means a paying proposition. He needs that. He paid $2½ million for the Alkali. Later this evening, we will examine one of the old deeds which shows 160 prime acres of the home place selling to one of the original owners for a five-dollar bill.

We walk up to the big house built by a previous owner (four-teen bedrooms, eight bathrooms), under the linden trees, imported from Europe, and talk about this historic piece of ground.

The name itself puzzles many. There is a lake near the big house called Alkali Lake but it is not and never has been an alkali lake. Turns out the first settler called this Paradise Valley. Men walking the trail to the Cariboo goldfields remembered it better by the prominent white alkali scar on the valley's northern face and called it Alkali Valley. In time the name transferred to the lake and to the ranch.

Herman Otto Bowe, a Frisian from Helgoland who had mined in California and at Barkerville, preempted land here on March 19, 1863, and the next year drove 500 head of Texas longhorn up from the Oregon territory to start the ranch.

This apparently makes it the oldest ranch in Canada. Plenty of farmers kept cattle for beef long before that but as parts of farm operations. Of the true, open-range cattle ranch, this one is rated as the original. It is at least a more probable claim than that the Gang Ranch is the biggest ranch in the world. You could drop twenty Gang Ranches into some of the northern Australian ranches and not be able to find them.

Herman Bowe came first; Henry Bowe, his son, second. C. W. Wynn-Johnson bought the Alkali in 1909 and sold in 1939 to Mario von Riedemann. Mario died and was succeeded by his son Martin Riedemann, who died of hypothermia after upsetting in the lake during a Halloween fireworks party.

In 1976, Doug and Marie Mervyn had just sold their big ski operation outside Kelowna. They bought and moved into the big house that had been built in the time of Mario, a handsome place but depressingly large, says Marie, particularly with three of the four children grown and gone.

Although Doug had herded sheep for a year, when young and footloose, he did not know much about ranching. "What I had and what I kept was the Riedemann's manager, Bronc Twan. He has a few cowboys, according to the season, but not many any more. Although we still do have a cowboy bunkhouse on this place."

Doug and Marie both cowboy and do all the many manners of work available for using up your time on a ranch. The day, it is said, is usually done before Doug is.

The surprise of the evening's conversation is to discover history making a neat, circular turn here on the Alkali. Doug Mervyn, who after nine years has developed some firm ideas of his own, is making a partial return to the Texas longhorn stock of the last century. His cows are Hereford, with some of the exotic Simmental, but most of his bulls are longhorn.

"There's more than one reason. The shoulders are smaller and the cows give birth easier. We used to have twenty to thirty Caesarean births a year. Last year we didn't have one. The meat is leaner. I think the animals are hardier. After all, the longhorn developed here on this continent out of feral Spanish cattle."

It is Doug's conviction that most cattlemen have lost touch with their customers. They are wedded to the idea of blocky whitefaces, larded with fat. "But the customer doesn't want fat anymore. He wants lean meat."

In Wyoming, he says, ranchers on an experimental program increased sales by more than 50 per cent by raising meat called Wyoming Lean, twenty-two to twenty-four months old, exclusively grass-fed.

The beef industry has got to stop producing six billion pounds of unwanted fat every year, says the newest owner of the oldest ranch. Next morning the animals are still bawling.

"Another two days and they'll quit complaining," says Doug. *There* is a difference from corporation executives. If cut off from a government subsidy, their squawling has only begun at the end of three days.

The Man Who Built
the Sky Ranch

BIG CREEK—There are three monuments to Gus Piltz in this country—the Sky Ranch, Piltz's Peak, and the Piltz Foundation. To those who met the man only occasionally and casually, finding him just another dour old rancher, they may each seem oversize. Yet there they stand, monuments.

Of them, the greatest creation is Sky Ranch. It is a carpet of grass laid in a shallow pass between the Gaspard Creek ranges of the mighty Gang Ranch and the scattered wild hay meadows of the Big Creek country. It is a mile high, higher than any ranch has a right to be at this latitude.

People used to say it was the highest ranch in the world. You may be sure this is untrue. So are almost all other claims about ranches which are the biggest, the wettest, the farthest north or south, or the richest. People just like to say such things about ranches.

What is true is that Sky Ranch consistently produced prize-winning lots of cattle at Williams Lake and that at one time it ran 550 head of stock, a very large herd in a country designed for grizzly bears and swamp moose.

Sky Ranch was built by the tenacity, the drive, the determination, perhaps the genius of one man, who devoted one lifetime to it.

August Martin Piltz came to Canada from a German colony in Czarist Russia. His own family couldn't get out of the Ukraine until later and Gus was smuggled in on the passport of a family named Wersh. He had to teach himself to read and write English, and in the great new land we were then he was apparently fitted for nothing more than labour. He began cowboying here in 1912 for Joe Tretheway of Chilco Ranch.

In 1917 he settled on the piece of ground which was to become the Sky Ranch. At that time it was called Big Swamp. He trapped, bought a few heifers on credit and, in 1918, began forty years of ceaseless work. He drained that swamp.

First he channelled it, hoping the water would run away down Coopering Creek. It didn't. If Gus was dismayed, he was also undaunted. He cut a ditch around the entire perimeter of the swamp, carrying away the mountains' runoff before it could reach the flat land. That worked, but it took more than most men have the muscle or the mind for.

The toughness of Gus Piltz has nourished more yarns in these parts than the man would have had time to live. One will do for an example.

Riding back to his little cabin one night on a half-wild cayuse (all the Piltz horses were half wild) he galloped into a wire clothes line, took out all his teeth, and rearranged half the bones of his face.

He was unconscious for some time. When he got off the ground he went to the cabin, examined his wrecked face, and tucked together the broken bones by hand as well as he could. Then he fainted again.

He revived, caught another horse and rode, all that night and much of the next day, almost 50 miles to the first aid post at Alexis Creek. Being Gus Piltz, he left a note on the Church Ranch gate, 18 miles from Sky Ranch. He had been feeding cattle for Church that winter. He wanted them to know that the cows would be untended for a day or two.

Later he hired help. They seldom stayed long. He was demanding, irascible, sometimes plain mean.

To have lived on moosemeat and huckleberries through the Hungry Thirties was one thing. To hired help of the 1950s it was less understandable that the man who raised prize beef felt he couldn't afford to have both butter and jam on the table at the same time.

When I first visited him in the fifties he served a hot rum. I should have been satisfied that it was not his other favourite drink which was whisky and Cherry Heering mixed in equal parts. I asked if he had any sugar for the rum. "You'll drink it that way," said Gus.

A nephew, Leonard Gildner of Portland, worked for him in 1945. "I got away from there as soon as I had a stake enough to get. He was a hard man to work for. But, then, he is my uncle, my own flesh and blood. He is me and I am him."

Gus never married. He courted the beautiful Hattie Hance, but she chose Frank Witte. For the rest of his life Gus had a particular love for Hattie's children and he was a regular Sunday visitor at the Witte's Circle A ranch on the creek.

That was another Piltz characteristic. He never worked on Sundays. Neither did any man or woman in his employment. It wasn't for religious reasons because he had little if any religious faith. It was the Piltz way.

The nephew, Leonard Gildner, bears testimony to those Sunday excursions to the Circle A.

"As we rode downhill, Gus got gentler and friendlier. By the time we arrived at Circle A, he was a real human being. When we rode back up the mountain at night, he got meaner and meaner and by the time we were at the Sky Ranch he was the same old sonofabitch."

He read avidly and liked discussing politics and all the other ideas of educated men. But he never undertook guiding, packing or other sidelines by which the district ranchers padded their thin incomes. He was a rancher only.

Oddly enough, although acclaimed a good rancher, he was never considered a good cowboy. He rode recklessly, but without grace or style, and he broke many bones.

The last bunch were broken by a horse in 1957. He sold the ranch and moved into Williams Lake.

Suddenly, Gus Piltz found himself with what was, for the 1950s, a modest fortune.

Singlemindedly, he set out to give it away. He provided a few bequests for relatives and friends and had almost $100,000 left. With this he created the Piltz Foundation which gives annual grants to children seeking the education that Gus never got.

With alarming speed he lapsed into senility. Some said it was because the new owners had run an air strip across one of the best hay meadows on Sky Ranch.

He lived on for dim years in a private hospital and finally died January 23, 1967.

The Piltz Foundation money still goes out, year after year. This fall there were fifty-three applicants. The income from the $100,000 fund provided grants for twenty-two.

Gus is buried at the Lake.

He had told his nephew that he was to be buried on the mountain behind the ranch. It was all written down, he said. But when he died there was nothing written down that could be found.

That mountain is Piltz's Peak on our maps. It rises, green-timbered at the base, bare grey rock at the top, above what used to be called Big Swamp. It is not particularly high or graceful, but it is solid, unchanging, enduring.

Ollie Nikolaye,
Who Was Loved

ANAHIM LAKE—He was born Johnnie Robertson, his Indian name was *Nookelow*, and by some process of change that would be difficult to trace, he spent his life under the name Ollie Nikolaye.

By any standards, including the rather hard standards of the frontier, Ollie was given a poor start in life. His mother was an Indian and his father a white. His father died of gunshot in the Nmiah Valley, just about the time that the boy was born. His mother struggled along with the child for a few years. But when he was about ten, she gave him away to an Indian named Little Johnnie, a cowboy of the Tatla Lake Ranch.

Little Johnnie did his best for Ollie. For clothing, he bought him a suit of men's overalls, full size. The legs had to be cut off almost at the crotch to let the child's feet reach the ground, and the overalls were so big around the waist that they almost made a complete double-wrap when cinched up with a large belt. All cowboys agreed that little Ollie was about the most comical looking kid that the country could provide.

Little Johnnie was killed near Pinto Lake when thrown from his horse during the fall roundup. The other cowboys shot the offending horse and packed Little Johnnie back to the ranch on a packhorse.

105

There was an element of coincidence in the death of Little Johnnie. Pinto Lake is today one of the favourite haunts of Ollie's half-sister, who is nicknamed *Chee Wit* (The Chickadee). She lives in the bush most of the time—as wild, almost, as the deer. But this was all to come much later.

That autumn day, Ollie's childhood came to an official end. The only father he ever knew was dead, and it was time for him to work for his living. He lived for a time with Old Sulin at Morrison Meadow near here, then at the Three Circle Ranch, then at many other ranches. Ollie did not turn to rape, arson, and pillage, as is supposed to be common among people of such a deprived childhood. Instead, he developed all those qualities which are most highly prized in the cattle country.

He had immense endurance. His word was good. He loved adventure. He could work hard and play hard. He could fight, and over the years accumulated a gunshot wound and a knife scar.

He was a witty man, and could tell a better story in broken English than many a fluent man. The stories lose something in cold print, but some of the man's flair shows even in this fragment:

"When we come out of them jack pine, that grizzly bear ain't at that moose carcass any more. He has come around behind us and he is standing up on his hind legs behind that American. I say to that American, I say, 'I think you turn 'round, you see that bear he's close enough for pictures now.'

"Me, I put my gun on that bear's head. I say, 'I think you should hurry up them pictures.' But the American don't say nothing. I don't know what he's doing. I got no looks to give to that American, I got all my looks for that grizzly bear. Sure funny thing, that bear. He's got his mouth open, just like he's laughin' about something. I keep telling that man better he take them pictures fast, but he don't answer.

"After a little time, that bear goes away and then I look for that hunter. Funny thing, he ain't there at all. He is running. He is almost all the way back up the hill to that camp we got. All that time, I been just talkin' to myself."

Ollie married twice and had children. He never acquired his own ranch, nor did he ever learn to read or write. But luck was good enough to him. When he lost his saddle in a poker game, he could be expected to win it back with a set of chaps in addition at the next game. One year, he lost his trap line in a horseshoe-pitching contest, but won it back the following year. Win or lose, his high good humour never changed.

Finally, in 1960, his luck ran out. He was setting choker on a logging show in the Bella Coola valley. The radio whistles were then just being introduced and something went wrong with one. A log crushed the life out of him.

He is buried at the Anahim Lake Indian Reserve cemetery, where some of the graves have little houses built over them. His tombstone is of granite. It says: "Ollie Nikolaye, 1906–1960, Died in Bella Coola. Rest in Peace."

The measure of the man, however, is not his rather expensive and formal grave marker, but in the powerful memories he has left in this region. Scarcely a man does not have a story to tell about the great Ollie Nikolaye, and all of these stories are told with respect and affection. His death is still deplored as a sinful waste. The death of kings has been forgotten in far less time here.

The Father of the Groom

—A very successful wedding has just been held here. There was organ music, confetti, a bride and bridesmaids as fair as the dawn, and a big bowl of punch at the Elks Hall.

Weddings don't just happen. People have to plan them. Not enough of us appreciate this, and it is about time that some of us did. Consider, in this matter, the dressing of the Father of the Groom.

His name is Lester Dorsey. He has been ranching for forty-odd years in the Anahim Lake country. He has many horses. Many, many horses. In fact, many, many, many horses. Some of the LD brand are feeding almost as far east as Alexis Creek. He has many friends, even though he is an old rancher.

Although Pan Phillips held over at Quesnel, and some of the other Chilcotin men had to stay home to feed stock, a great many other friends of the Father of the Groom came to the wedding. They were earnestly intent on doing their bit to make it a success. It was decided by these friends that the Father of the Groom should wear a white shirt with a stiff collar. Also a necktie. The necktie, made of cloth, was purchased at Burkowski's store. It was coloured more or less like latigo, but was cheaper and softer. A Forsythe shirt was obtained at Mackenzie's store.

The dressing of the Father of the Groom took place in Room 218 of the Lakeview Hotel. Randolph Mulvahill of Chezacut helped to hold him down. The Father of the Groom had, by God, never worn a white shirt and tie in his life, and before he did, Hell would freeze solid from shore to shore. Even then, he said, he was prepared to sit around on the ice for a spell first.

Some furniture got overturned. A cowboy named George sat on his legs and Mike Dorsey, Brother of the Groom, also helped.

After Mr. Dorsey had been placed inside the boiled shirt, and the necktie had been cinched up tight against his Adam's apple, which is rather like an old pine-tree knot, his friend Mr. Mulvahill became sentimental about the whole business.

Mr. Mulvahill said that he had never realized that his friend L. Dorsey, Father of the Groom and holder of the LD horse brand, had such a natural elegance about him. Clearly, said Mr. Mulvahill, Mr. Dorsey had missed his calling. He should have been a stockbroker in Vancouver, or even Toronto.

Mr. Mulvahill spoke sadly of his own condition, that of a poor, simple Chilcotin rancher who still wore his pants inside his boot-tops. Here he was, he said, obliged to attend this wedding in an open-neck blue shirt and jeans.

Mr. Mulvahill offered to go away into a dark corner of the hotel and sit there all night, worrying about this. Mr. Dorsey said that Mr. Mulvahill could go right ahead and do that very thing.

Mr. Mulvahill then spoke with deep sincerity of the days when his friend Lester rode seventy-five miles across the mountains to the Mulvahill ranch, wearing an open-neck shirt and thin coat and scarcely anything more, surviving the most vicious winter weather by sheer strength of character. Times had changed, said Mr. Mulvahill.

The Father of the Groom was put into a suit. A white

handkerchief was placed in the upper left front pocket. There was applause. The Father of the Groom was dusted, combed, and heavily advised.

Randolph Mulvahill wept, on behalf of himself, an ordinary rancher to whom the fused collar and the reversible cuff were unknown. He suggested that his good friend, the Father of the Groom, once an ordinary rancher like himself, should now slowly wean himself from that lowly estate. He suggested that Mr. Dorsey might next keep milk cows. From that he could go to sheep. He would then be ready to become an insurance salesman or bank manager or some other damn thing of that sort.

The Father of the Groom was escorted away from Room 218 and he went to the church and sat there quietly, thinking thoughts that are not known to us.

The Lakeview management plan to put up a small plaque over Room 218. Nothing gaudy. Just a small piece of bronze. It will say:

This is the Room
Where Lester Dorsey of the Anahim Country
Got into a White Shirt and Tie
For the First Time

With all this planning, the wedding was, of course, a success.

When the wedding was over, Lester gave me back the shirt and tie. He said once was enough.

The management knew nothing of those events in Room 218 until they read my newspaper column some time later. To make an honest man of me, they had the bronze plaque made up and tacked it to the door. It was stolen and they put up another, and then another. But the plaques kept getting pinched so after a while they gave up and now there is hardly a guest who passes through that establishment who can tell where history was made.

110

The Man with
the Extra Airport

BIG CREEK—Within the tight circle of my friends, the number who have become wealthy remains discouragingly small. For some time, I have thought that none of us will make it.

However, this has now been changed. Bruce Watt has become one of the wealthiest men in B.C. The rest of us may now take heart and try again, casting our thought nobly beyond the meager affairs of grocery bills and payments on the car.

Bruce has, I suppose, been wealthy for some years. But we had not noticed. Perhaps we were misled by the fact that he doesn't have much money.

We did not notice that he was, in fact, rich beyond the dreams of most men. By this I do not mean that he had his health. Health is not wealth, despite what some may claim. Consider how many healthy men are living on welfare cheques.

No, the attainment of opulence is marked sometimes by money, sometimes by an action of some grandeur. A symbol becomes visible, a symbol such as cannot be produced by ordinary men, only by those who are wealthy.

Bruce's abounding wealth became visible in early October this year, at which time it became apparent that somebody had built an airport in his front yard and he hadn't even noticed. I happened to be visiting Breckness Ranch on the day that the news broke. Bruce was not behaving like a wealthy man on that day. He was rummaging his log house for his good pair of pants. He planned to go to Williams Lake, and although he is a man with no more passion for personal daintiness than most of us, he felt that it would be nice to go clad in good pants. And he only owns one pair.

He had learned that day, he said, that somebody had built a damn' airport at his Dry Farm—the summer range he occupies near the junction of the Chilcotin and Fraser rivers. He didn't know who and he didn't know why, but he intended to look into the matter.

That day he went to the Lake wearing his old pants, which are torn in the seat and at the crotch.

A few days later we made our separate ways to the Dry Farm and there found that, sure enough, somebody had built an airfield on Bruce's Crown Grant land. Not on his grazing area, not on some piece of open range where his rights are of a more tenuous sort—but on his own personal property, right in front of the big log house where he and his family live when they are operating this end of his small ranch.

Big equipment had been used. The hollows had been filled and the hills levelled by great earth-movers. The big airstrip ran 2000 feet through his grass—big, raw, bare, and fit to carry anything up to the size of a DC-3. The equipment had departed and so had the crews. But the men who built the field had apparently helped themselves to Bruce's house, and its kitchen was a mess.

Now, how does a wealthy man react when he discovers that somebody has built an airfield in his yard without asking his permission, has messed up his house, destroyed some of his grass, and left without saying thank you. It was plain that these thoughts were going through the man's mind. You could tell, by his serious expression, that he was thinking. After a while he spoke. "By God, Paul, you know, I think maybe I ought to get hostile about this."

That was two months ago. Last week I drove in to Big Creek to discover how hostile Bruce had become. Well, he said, he had been thinking about it. There was something about a man coming on your property without your permission, using your house, breaking your fences, and putting an airport in your front yard that tended to irritate a man. One of these days, he said, he was maybe going to do something about it.

He still owns only one pair of good pants and he still hasn't found them.

After writing this column I became disturbed. Bruce was, after all, an old friend who might be in some legal difficulties. I took the column to his wife, Phyllis. She was then living in Williams Lake, so that the numerous Watt offspring might attend school. Splitting the family is often a routine of ranch life. There may be no other method of combining children with education.

"Bruce may want to sue some mining company on this matter," I said. "Maybe I had better not run it."

"That's the way he is," she said. "It's a good column." I was reassured, but not by that much.

I drove for a few hours to Bruce's home ranch and, after a few more hours of waiting, he came home.

"You had better read this column, Bruce," I said. "If you are going to sue, it might interfere with the court case."

We ate macaroni and cheese, his favourite and almost exclusive dish, and he read the column.

"That's the way it was," he said.

"But will it interfere in a lawsuit?"

"What the hell," he said, "it's the way it was. You ought to print it."

If Bruce has a second pair of pants, I have been kept in ignorance. But he sure in hell has enough airports.

Looking for Horses

Because so much of my travel was in the ranch country, horses were a subject that constantly recurred. Some readers even got the impression that I liked horses. Personally, I can conceive of a life which is full, rich, and rewarding and which has nothing to do with horses. On the occasions when I have been obliged to use them, it was in the spirit that second-class riding is better than first-class walking.

But generations of cattlemen seem to feel otherwise about these animals, and although the economic theory is that ranchers keep horses only because they need them to handle cattle, I have met a few whom I suspect keep cattle only as an excuse for running horses.

In any event, throughout much of the Chilcotin, horses replace weather as a means of opening conversation.

BIG CREEK—A few days ago, when it was twelve below up at the Teepee Heart Ranch, Duane Witte suggested that we go looking for horses. Well, I was delighted, of course. As a matter of fact, I didn't really mind very much. Here was a chance to take part in one of the esoteric rites of the Cariboo: looking for horses.

In the Cariboo, it does not matter where a stranger comes to rest, or why. He may be in a moose camp or a duck blind. He may be prospecting or taking pictures of kigli holes. If he but wait a little while, a rider will come by and this rider will say that he is looking for horses.

Sometimes I have told these riders that yes, I did see some horses that day, and have described the horses. Sometimes I have been able to describe the brand. Sometimes I have not seen any horses. One answer appears to please a rider as much as another. He is very grateful for the information, and says, "Thank you," and then says that he must be off again looking for horses, and he leaves.

So last Thursday, for the first time, I was introduced to this mystery as a rider, one of the people who ask the questions.

Shortly after noon, when it was warm, we left the ranch. Duane and his wife, Marian, rode young paints and I was on an elderly bay, sometimes used to pack moose. The snow lay deep and crusted, and the moose, who were rustling for food in the horse pasture, paused in brushing the snow away with their long forelegs and watched us go by. They appeared to wonder what we were doing. But moose have a naturally puzzled expression, anyway, and possibly they were not really interested at all.

By 1:30 P.M. we had seen two Stellar's jays, three chickadees, one whisky jack, and a Franklin's grouse cock, who came out from beneath the horse's feet with a blast of powdered snow, more like a cannon than a rocket. At 2:00 P.M. we sighted half a dozen horses on one of the long buckbrush meadows of Duane's ranch. They were pawing in the snow for feed, as the moose had been doing—and, like the moose, they paused to look at us as we went past. They were Duane's horses. Unfortunately, they were not the ones he was looking for.

We saw coyote track, lynx track, rabbit track, moose track, and squirrel track. Even our stirrups left tracks as our horses walked through the deeper snows.

There were some of Duane's horses on the meadow that we reached at 3:00 P.M. But these also were not the ones that he was looking for.

Duane rode right to look over a spruce swamp, and Marian and I went to the Big Meadow. We found horses in both places. But these too were not the right ones.

We rode by an old corral built by wild-horse hunters. (Hunting horses is much different from looking for horses. But that is another story.) We rode through the little grove of trees where the rustlers had camped a few years ago. They stole thirty horses from Duane and are believed to have driven them north to the roadless ranges above his ranch.

When it was late in the afternoon, an east wind began to cut at our cheekbones with little pieces of broken razor blade, and we came home to the ranch house. We had seen, oh, quite a lot of horses, I would say, although not one of those that we had set out to look for. And that is what it is all about.

The only thing I forgot to find out was why we were looking for them. The thought did not occur to me until a day later, when I was hours away on the road out to Hanceville.

Come to think of it, in all the years of meeting riders in the Cariboo, I have never met one who found his horses, nor one who said why he wanted to find them. What an opportunity was mine! I could have penetrated to the very heart of the mystery! There I was, riding with the man. He was there. An expert. All I had to do was ask the question. But I never asked him.

That is the way a man fritters away the great opportunities of life.

Looking for Horses Again

BIG CREEK—The last couple of days have been spent at Duane Witte's Teepee Heart Ranch in the Cariboo. We were looking for horses. I don't know why. But there is, no doubt, some reason.

Duane's place is at the Eight Mile Meadow. It is eight miles beyond what was traditionally considered the end of the road. However, it is now possible to drive a car to Duane's except for some periods of spring, winter, summer, and fall. A couple of days ago, it was possible—and there, in the yard of his ranch, was Duane. He was fixing the tractor and thinking about horses.

"I am pretty sure," he said, "that my good team is up at the Long Jim Meadow."

The Long Jim being only twenty miles distant, we decided to ride over there to look for the team. What we would do if we found them he did not say. Drive them down to the corral where we could have a good look at them before turning them loose again, perhaps. Something of that sort.

First, however, to save a day's ride, we made a trip down the trail to the Bell Ranch. Sherwood Henry is on the Bell Ranch. Sherwood probably had been in touch with Lynn Bonner of the Deer Creek Ranch. Lynn has a plane. Possibly he had been flying over the range. Possibly he had seen Duane's horses. Possibly he had told Sherwood about it. Think of the time we'd save.

So we drove out of Eight Mile and went down the road and didn't get stuck until we hit the hill on Jack's Mountain. We had to put chains on, and this took two hours because the chains didn't fit. Putting small chains on large wheels requires a great deal of perseverance, deep in the night with no flashlight, and we were very late waking up Sherwood at the Bell Ranch. It didn't matter, however, because although Lynn had been flying, he hadn't flown over the Long Jim Meadow so there wasn't a thing that Sherwood could tell us about Duane's horses.

This ended the first day of the horse hunt.

On the second day, many people had collected at the Teepee Heart Ranch. Harold Nickson of the Old Hutch Place had come to fix Duane's tractor. Lonnie Russel of the Anvil Mountain Ranch, another neighbour, had come to help. Thus, there were plenty of riders—ample to hunt for horses on the Long Jim. However, there weren't enough saddle horses in the corral for all of us. So before riding up to Long Jim to hunt horses, we had first to hunt Duane's saddle horses. They were feeding nearby on Wild Horse Range and Big Opening.

I declined this exercise. Harold, Lonnie, Duane, and his wife, Marian, went out for the saddle horses shortly after noon. Harold, Lonnie, and Marian were home by dark. They hadn't found the saddle horses. The horses had moved for some reason. Why, nobody knew.

Duane got home at nine. His spurs jingled like Santa Claus' bells when he stepped on the porch, but he wasn't noticeably cheerful. His face had been cut by brush. It is hard to chase horses through jack pine in the dark of a moonless winter night. He had cut track. His saddle horses were moving west for some reason. They were probably heading for Bald Mountain. He didn't know why.

Duane was riding Colonel Ambleman, his Tennessee-walking horse stud. The stud could detect the stepping holes of the other horses in the snow long after Duane had lost sight of them. But eventually even Colonel Ambleman couldn't follow the trail any longer, so they had come home.

On the third day of the horse hunt, Duane, Harold, and Lonnie set out to find the saddle horses with which we were to look for the other horses which were possibly up at Long Jim Meadow. The saddle horses are probably on Bald Hill Mountain. Either that or they have gone over the watershed to Paxton Valley. If they are in Paxton Valley, it will take—oh, a long time—to get them back.

Unfortunately, I can't wait. I must pull out tonight. However, I am in the third day of hunting horses and I have not yet had to climb aboard a single knot-headed cayuse. It is one of the best horse hunts I have ever attended. And just as productive as any other.

Mustangs and Other Horses

ALEXIS CREEK—The fickle eye of public interest has, in recent years, focussed briefly on the Cariboo wild horses. Wild horses have attracted the attention of ranchers for generations, but the interest of the general public in such matters is always briefer—although it may be, for a short time, far more intense.

The majority view of the ranchers seems clear. They want wild horses tamed, trapped, and sold, or shot, according to merit. They do not want them on their ranges. They say that they are runts which kidnap mares from domestic herds and take them away into the mountains. They say that wild horses breed down the domestic stock. They say that the life of a wild horse is nasty, brutish, and short—and the shorter the better.

Those who love the wild horse bands say there is something splendid about anything wild and free. Should we wipe out the last of the wild horse bands, they say, we will regret it, even as we would regret the extinction of moose, deer, or any other wild creature.

Having had the good fortune to watch a wild band stampeding across a lonely mountain meadow with their broomtails streaming in the wind of their passage, I have been able to develop a sympathy for both points of view. Hence the following observations, which prove nothing.

Much of the argument as to what constitutes a wild horse is spurious. Those who like them maintain that they are the original mustangs which flooded the western plains of North America after the Spaniards introduced the horse to this continent in the seventeenth century. Those who dislike them say that the Cariboo herds are simply domestic stock, run wild. It may be argued that both are correct.

The word mustang is from the old Spanish word *mestana,* which means a domestic animal that has escaped the control of its original owner. In Mexico, the words *mestano* and *mestana* were applied to the stallions and mares that went wild. In later years, Mexican ranchers substituted the name *marron* for wild stock, but in the United States the name mustang clung. The modern domestic horse that runs wild is repeating the pattern of the Mexican ranch stock. Whether the name mustang applies is an academic argument.

As to type, most western ranch horses are descended from the Spanish-Barb stocks. Many types developed. Some, such as the Appaloosa and the Paint, have been standardized for registration during this century, after having long been lumped together under general names such as Indian pony or cayuse.

In the Cariboo, the name wild horse may occasionally be applied to domestic stock that has been left on the range after the closure date in late fall or winter. Usually it is applied to bands of horses that have run uncontrolled for years and have bred generations of unbranded animals. They are of all colours and shapes, but successive generations become smaller and may tend to become dark of colour with the so-called wild stripe on the backbone. The rule of thumb in distinguishing wild horses is their immense growth of mane and tail, the hair of the latter sweeping the grass as they walk. Hence the name broomtail.

Only in the narrowing area of the West that is given over to open-range ranching does the question of wild horse control exist, with the exception of a few isolated groups such as the wild ponies of Sable Island. However, in the Cariboo, the division between wild and tame horses becomes almost indistinguishable. On most ranges, the grazing division of the Forestry Department insists that domestic stock be brought off the open range in winter. Those remaining on the range may be killed (in some areas) despite the fact that they are branded animals.

Wild horse herds develop during cycles of moderate weather. In the late 1940s, ranchers say that a band of at least five hundred roamed the region of Sugar Loaf Mountain near Anahim Lake. The desperate winters of 1949 and 1950 are believed to have eliminated them all. Those who are opposed to the protecting of wild horses say that it is an exercise in cruelty, that in the B.C. mountains all such bands face a cruelly slow death by starvation when one of our severe winters locks up their feed areas in the remote mountain valleys.

Over the years, the wild-horse herds have been thinned by men as well as by winters. Hunting is always done in winter. Some herds are driven into crudely built corrals with long wings. Once trapped there, animals of good conformation may be chosen for domestication. Others may be sold into the United States to be butchered for fox feed.

In other circumstances, cowboys are sent out to shoot wild horses. Bounties are sometimes paid for wild horses, the hunters bringing a set of ears for a mare's bounty or ears and testicles to claim stallion's bounty. It is said that in years past, some hunters found the game department willing to accept moose testicles with mares' ears and that the kill of wild horse stallions reached astounding proportions. This might be true.

No matter what the activity of the hunters or protectionist societies, it seems safe to predict that wild horse bands will exist for many years in B.C. They are continually being reconstituted from domestic stock.

However, as the fences advance and our wilderness shrinks, we may encounter a day when they will no longer exist. Whether this will be a better and kinder thing is still open to debate.

On Old Horses,
Winter, and Death

ALEXIS CREEK—Some of us were sitting around talking the other night when the subject of horses arose.

This is winter, when the old gentleman with the scythe passes among the horse herds, making his selections. These selections are usually made among the young and the old horses, for slightly different reasons.

Colts and yearlings do not endure winter as well as mature horses. Some ranchers estimate that only fifty per cent of young horses survive to the age of five. They are inexperienced, more prone to falling into spring holes and to other hazards. Also, their inability to endure severe cold has a simple arithmetical explanation. Young animals have a larger ratio of skin area to bulk. Thus, their body heat dissipates quicker. Sometimes they cannot eat enough to fuel their little bodies against the steady drain of cold.

At about twenty-five another process operates, one less easily explained, except in the two simple words—old age. These old horses may have done their accustomed work in summer and may have fattened satisfactorily in the golden days of autumn. But they will fade during the long winter.

Even if fed grain, these old pensioners who once rustled for themselves will become gaunt as the winter progresses. The snow will lie on their backs. Some will be cast in the snow—unable to rise from a fold of the ground where they have carelessly lain to sleep—and if they do struggle to their feet again they may rise with one side frozen. Ranchers can usually apprehend, before autumn ends, when a horse is facing his last winter. They then sell the old animal to be slaughtered for fox feed, or they shoot him.

We were talking of such gloomy matters here last night with Lester Dorsey of Anahim Lake. He was passing through town with more than his usual speed, the back of his pickup laden with sacks of grain. On Lester's range there has been heavy snow, then rain, and then a freeze. These are the classic conditions of a mass starve-out and he was in great haste to take feed into those ice-bound meadows.

Last fall, he had forty pack horses and saddle horses in his hunting territory behind the Rainbow Mountains. When the last of his hunters left, Lester looked over the herd and selected those whose work had ended. With one of his guides, he led them one by one down the meadow and shot them. They were Red, Brownie, Little Joe, Dago Pete, Old Alec, and Shanaham.

"I would never sell an old horse for fox feed," he said. "I saw some of those old horses in the yards at Kamloops one time. They were being shipped down to the States to be butchered. I decided right then that it didn't matter how hard things ever got for me, I would never need twenty bucks enough to sell an old horse for fox feed.

"Shooting them used to bother me. Years ago, I used to hire fellows to shoot them for me. But I went out in the meadow one night and found an old horse that had been shot in the afternoon and he was still alive. So that ended that. I always shot my own after that.

"Still, it used to bother me a lot, up until just a few years ago. Then I began to feel differently about it. You just take the heaviest gun in camp—my Ought-Six is pretty good—bring it up fast, just between the eyes, and pull. Usually, there's only one kick when they go down.

"I don't believe they ever know what's happening. They're old anyhow, and it all happens too fast for them to know what is coming. Just *Bang* and they're down, and there are no more hard winters."

So we agreed that we all have to go some time, which is probably the tritest statement of the human condition that can be made.

"In our case," said Lester, "when we die, somebody who never knew us will make a nice speech about us. You may be the lowest type man the country has ever produced, but somebody will say something nice about you. And they'll give you a bunch of flowers that you can't smell. Quite a thing to look forward to, ain't it?"

The Wild Horse Hunter

REDSTONE—A conversation with Gay Bayliff of the Chilahnko Ranch turned to the subject of horses. Gay used to shoot them—for pay, as well as for the good of his range.

Gabriel Thomas Bayliff is the second of four generations on this ranch, all of whom have retained some English accent. The first in Chilcotin was Hugh, who swam his first cattle across the Fraser near the Gang in 1887. Gabriel, now the eldest of the B.C. clan, edged into retirement during recent years. He serves as a stipendiary magistrate at nearby Alexis Creek. One son of the third generation, Tony, owns and operates the Newton Ranch, which adjoins Chilahnko Ranch. The other son, Tim, has Chilahnko. Tim lives in the big brown Edwardian mansion that was built by Hugh.

Horses can never be far from their thoughts. Tony is recovering from a severe bruising. A week ago, he was pinned under his horse when it fell on ice. Tim's daughter, Elizabeth, is encased in plaster from head to hips. Her horse ran away during a game of hide-and-seek with some other children and her neck was broken.

Near the original family home, Gabriel and his wife, Dorothy, have built a small, modern home. It was there that we were talking, over tea and fine biscuits, and Mr. Bayliff recalled his days as

127

a horse hunter. He does not believe that wild western horses preceded the white man in Chilcotin. His father said that the Chilcotin Indians had no horses in the 1880s. Also, notes Mr. Bayliff, an early missionary has recorded that the Indians had no word for horse. They referred to Hudson's Bay men as elkmen, in reference to their use of the horse.

The 1930s was one of several periods in which much domestic stock went wild on these ranges. Mr. Bayliff was one of those hired as government hunters.

"I didn't shoot any extraordinary number. Nothing to compare with Johnnie Henderson, who must have shot well over four hundred during those years. I would say the most I ever shot in one year would be seventy-five."

He was paid seventy-five dollars a month to hunt wild horses and got a bounty for each scalp, the amount of which he cannot recall with certainty. He thinks it was one dollar for each mare's scalp and two dollars for the scalp and testicles of stallions.

"They were always in bands. At first, I was advised to kill the stallion first, but I soon learned that that was wrong. When they were alarmed, the stallion would race around the edges of the band, nipping at his mares and colts to bunch them up. He would round them up and drive them. But it was always an old mare who led them.

"The method was to pick the leader and shoot her. The band would then mill around waiting for a new leader to move out in front and you'd have time for several more shots at them. Then, if you could kill the next leader, they'd stop again."

Hunting in this way, he was able to kill as many as eight horses in a single ambush.

"Your hope in tracking a band through timber was that you would catch them out on an open meadow where you could shoot. The stallion would hang back. He was the lookout. I don't know how many times I've tracked a band through the jack pines and never had any more success than hearing the stallion snort as he detected me and began driving them off."

He recalled a long and lonely hunt on a winter's day when he had outsmarted such a stallion by circling the band's tracks.

"When I got to the meadow, there he was, watching for me on their backtrail. I shot him with the 300 Savage and it was a good shot, a heart shot. I heard the bullet hit. He just kicked up his heels and began to round up his band as usual, racing around the edges, nipping and chivvying them. Then suddenly, he just somersaulted. He was dead before he hit the ground. In a sense, he was dead the moment the bullet hit him."

So we drank tea and looked out across the frozen valley of the Chilcotin and at the black hills of pine beyond where, now as formerly, a few horses returned each year to the wild.

"How he used to hate hunting horses," said Mrs. Bayliff. "How he used to hate it."

Horse Doctoring

BIG CREEK—A few of us were sitting around in a ranch-house kitchen the other night, just talking, when for some reason the conversation turned to the subject of horses. Horses have almost as many diseases as people. But when a horse is ailing, it may not be easy to tell which of the creature's ailments is temporarily in the ascendancy.

Many arguments arise from this situation. So in a very short time, our host went to his desk, which stands against the wall through which the moose has poked his head, and there found his good old reliable horse-doctor book. This little volume is five inches thick and weighs about as much as the average stock saddle. Needless to say, it contains the details of every malady known to the horse. Wind colic is there; also bots, contraction of the hoof, the strangles, pink eye, founder, galls, and glanders. There is plenty of material here for a long, long evening of melancholy discussion.

But there is more. The authors of *Vitalogy* (as my friend's horse-doctor book is titled) had a vision of world affairs extending far beyond the subject of horses. In fact, of the book's 1258 closely written pages, only 56 were devoted to horses. One might even suspect that my friend the rancher has misread the whole intent of *Vitalogy*. It is my opinion that the authors set out to write a book of comprehensive advice for humans and included 56 pages on horses as an afterthought. For humans, the advice offered is, to say the least, comprehensive.

Here, for instance, beginning at page 1231, is HOW TO SELECT A MATRIMONIAL PARTNER: "Don't marry a girl who hangs around drygoods and millinery stores," the authors say. "To dress extravagantly is a blot on any woman's character."

Now, how many of us had the benefit of advice such as this before our marriage? I ask, how many of us?

The authors of *Vitalogy* leave nothing to chance. They have included illustrations. There are two photographs showing suitable and unsuitable women. The unsuitable one is splendidly dressed (by the standards of 1890). She offers the promise, say the authors, of "a life of sorrow and sadness" for any man so unfortunate as to marry her. On the opposite page is a photograph of a suitable girl. She has a nose that would split hail stones and I personally do not find her attractive, but she is plainly dressed, which seems to be the important thing.

There is more, much more advice for humans in this old horse-doctor book. There is a remedy for hanging. The victim must be cut down, immediately (page 49).

Here is another interesting remedy for another condition: "Alcohol in any of its forms—brandy, whisky, gin, etc.—should be drunk largely by the patient. Let him drink freely, a gill or more at a time, once in fifteen or twenty minutes. Or small doses, oftener" (page 19). You might think this a cure for sobriety. You would be wrong. It is a specific for snake bites. (Kerosene oil may also be used, but the application is of less interest.)

Baldness? See page 771. The authors of *Vitalogy* have obtained the secret remedy of the royal house of Germany. "Burn the soles of cast-off shoes to a crisp, pulverize and mix with a small quantity of fresh lard, then apply at nights to the scalp lavishly." After a winter's treatment, you enter spring barefoot—but with any amount of hair on your head.

"I can't say that all the advice is sound," said our host. "There is one treatment there for a horse sickness which involves pouring one to two quarts of whisky into the horse. I have had some experience with that sickness and I have found it best to shoot the horse and drink the whisky for consolation."

With that, the conversation returned to the subject of horses, and all the other splendid advice available in *Vitalogy* was ignored. Those interested in other aspects of the book may buy their own copy. Publishers are Northern Publishing House of New York and Chicago. Unfortunately, the date of publication is 1900. It may be out of print by now.

Horses, Horses, Horses

WILLIAMS LAKE—*The following notes were taken from old ciga-rette packages, credit card receipts, corners torn from* Western Horseman, *and similar palimpsests. Some were hard to read, and possibly there is no truth in them. Who can say?*

"He was the best horse I ever owned. The best horse I ever will own. Maybe he was the best horse I ever deserved and maybe he was better than that.

"He was a wild horse. Dad and I trapped him in Dick Meadow when I was a kid. We took him home and broke him. I called him Satan.

"There is any number of things I could say about that horse, but I suppose at least half of them would be lies. It is true that I rode him sixty miles to a dance at the Gang one night, but lately when I have told this story it has stretched out to seventy and even ninety miles, so I suppose I am getting on to that age when the truth is hard to remember.

"One thing I can say in all truth about Satan. He had a tremendous dignity. Even after we had been together for years, I could never afford to ignore him. Why, when Satan was twenty years old and had been my horse all those years, I couldn't walk

133

up behind him without talking to him. If I did, he would still nail me with his heels.

"He could kick a man faster than any horse I have ever known. He could bite too. He was fast in every way.

"The important thing was, he had dignity. You could never take him for granted. You had to speak to him like an equal. Otherwise, he let you know that he was not an individual who could be taken casually.

"He was thirty-two when he died. He was the greatest horse I ever knew. I will never have another like him, but then I probably don't deserve to."

A former game guide speaks:

"We had some hunters back in the mountains and we ran into a wild-horse band. They were in a box canyon, so we spotted the hunters around the side and told them to shoot. Well, there is nothing wrong with that. We wanted to be rid of the wild horses. They shot them all down, the stallion, every mare, every colt. They were all down dead in the meadow.

"There is nothing wrong with shooting horses. I've shot lots of horses. But I was disgusted."

A rancher bringing saddle horses out of the corral for dudes to ride:

"That one? She's fine. She's been rode lots of times. The only trouble is, everybody who ever rides her gets bucked off."

Another rancher:

"He's fine to ride, but peculiar. He never bucks anybody off until he is at least five miles from home."

The greatest horses the Cariboo Country has ever produced are orphan colts. Orphan colts are found abandoned in spring holes and are hauled out with ropes, caked in mud of the consistency and tenacity of glue.

They are found—thin, knobby-kneed, stilt-legged—in empty meadows from which their mothers have been removed by the attention of bears or of a city hunter who cannot distinguish between a moose and his own grandmother.

These orphan colts are brought to the home place. They are fed milk and calf supplement by ranch wives. Ranch men stand at the back porch and expound on the vast potential of these little orphans. They distinguish in them all the best qualities of the quarter horse, Appaloosa, Arab, Barb, and Andalusian stocks from which they have sprung.

Given time, orphan colts grow up. As a rule, they turn out to be just another cayuse. They are turned out on the range and forgotten or, with luck, sold to the American who just bought the ranch next door. But the first year or two of their lives, they are visions of glory. Every place requires such visions from time to time. This may explain why the finding of an orphan colt is such an enjoyable experience.

What can compare with the vision of glory? Everybody needs one. This year's orphan colt may go, but another will be provided next year from the rich breast of nature and life will continue, nourished by hope.

Chilcotin's Last Great Horse

CHEZACUT—One of man's trials in visiting Chilcotin during the winter is that you are expected to admire everybody's damned old stud horse. It is a problem in the three other seasons also.

I have always said, "Yes, that is really a horse." It is a statement that is both honest and sincere and is usually good enough.

This trip, however, it happens that there has always been some neighbouring rancher present while the stud was being shown. What was once merely disinteresting became confusing, and if it weren't for a painter named Charley Russell my understanding of this mystery would be considerably less. I am grateful to the late Mr. Russell.

Over the week's earlier stud horse talk I draw a veil of sorts. I name no names. There is enough strife in this world.

We stopped the car in the Kleena Kleene area and looked into a corral where an Arab stud was reported to live. He was there and he was an Arab.

I never knew there was so much wrong with Arabs. They are dainty. They keep their heads too high and you can't see where you are going. They can't see themselves. They won't do.

At another ranch, we admired another stud. He looked like a dun but the owner said he was a buckskin.

It was a horse all right, but when the owner was not present a neighbour remarked, "Stud, hell, he wouldn't make a good gelding."

In the Anahim Lake country, the blood of the quarterhorse infuses stocks that would otherwise be known as cayuse. Privily, it was pointed out to me that these are Bulldog Quarterhorse, all right for cutting contests and other arena games but no good if you've got work to do farther than a quarter of a mile from the bunkhouse.

Once there was even criticism of a stud before the owner's face.

"I had two of these but I didn't need two so I sold one," said the owner. A neighbouring rancher told him, "If I had two studs like that, I would sell two of them."

It wasn't until coming here to Randolph Mulvahill's ranch—the Old Copeland Place, as it's called—that some of the mystery about great studs was blown away.

There are no great studs left in the Chilcotin, said Randolph. They are gone. All of them. All gone. There is none left. Not one. They are finished and done forever.

The great Chilcotin horses, he said, all originated with a Hamiltonian standardbred stud imported by one of the first big ranchers. It cost $6,000, at a time when that was a lot of money, and was resold years later to a Redstone Indian at $4,500.

Crossed with cayuse and Percheron, this fabulous sire spread strength, stamina, brains, and beauty over all the range west of the Fraser River.

The strain not merely petered out. It disappeared. There was a trace of the blood in his own stud, Randolph said. This might make his stud the best in the country but that wasn't saying much for it because the ancestor is so much greater.

Several of us were so instructed in the Mulvahill living room, which happens to be plastered, wall by wall, with Russell prints.

Russell outlived his rival Remington on Chilcotin ranch-house walls.

Remington's scenes were vibrant with action but Russell's, although often sentimental and sometimes melodramatic, have a detail that earns them undying respect from horsemen.

So it proved among the little band of ranchers gathered there that night.

Somebody's eye was caught by a Russell that depicts a bunch of cowboys riding over sagebrush hills in the American Southwest. One rode a big white horse.

Look at that for a horse, they said. A sliding blind at his eyes—he's so rank you can't get aboard him in the morning if he sees you first. And he's the only horse in the bunch with a hackamore; the others are all spade bitted.

As anybody could see, that horse had piled his rider just a few minutes before Charley painted the picture. There were spur gashes on his withers and there was blood on the rider's face.

There was some disagreement about whether the horse was just about to unwind again or if he had been bucked out into a passable gentleness for the rest of the day. It was all in the set of his legs and the way he held his head, and it was debatable, as you could tell by the way the rider held his lines.

There was no disagreement, none, that here was a truly great stud—mean, rank, treacherous, a horse that would carry a rider through all the fires of Hell and come out in the sunset of Eternity as snorty and as ornery as he was at the dawn.

So there is, you see, one truly great stud left in Chilcotin, but he is hanging on the wall of Randolph Mulvahill's living room.

Country People Don't Count

BIG CREEK—This little ranching community got its first phones in 1936 when the locals, resourceful as ever, strung some wires on the jack pines and connected to the outside world. Moose sometimes carried the wire off in their antlers, but the system worked a lot of the time.

After all, in 1936 talking to anybody by telephone was a bit special, and Grandad, who always shouted into the receiver when talking to somebody two hundred miles distant, would exclaim in wonder, "Why it sounded so clear you'd swear he was next door!" (Grandads never said that in Big Creek because Big Creek phones never sounded that clear, not even when the caller was next door, but let that pass for the moment.)

Now, it's 1999.

Mountaineers on Everest chat by phone to their families in Seattle and San Francisco. People talk back and forth to the moon. The arrival of the Internet on touch-tone telephones is changing the very foundations of society and caused a scientist to appear recently before a meeting of telephone executives, hold aloft a state-of-the-art telephone and announce, "This instrument is obsolete."

Meanwhile, back in Big Creek, they're still using dial telephones and listening to one another talk on party lines. They're forbidden to use Internet connections, phone answering machines or a lot of other devices which are normal to almost every home in Canada.

Since Big Creek no longer has a school, a store or even a post office in somebody's living room, you may well say, "So what if it's got funky old telephones? Big Creek is a small place. There are only a couple of hundred people in a 2500-square-kilometre place."

Know something? "So what?" is just about exactly what the people of Canada's cities and towns say to the few remaining rural regions of this country. The phone situation here is just one aspect of a far larger problem: the marginalization of country people.

Big Creek people have been petitioning the phone company year in and year out for the kind of phone service which is so common that it's verging on obsolescence in the rest of Canada. There are 40 such party-line-only communities in the province now, and Big Creek people say they should be at the top of the list for new service because almost all the others have at least paved roads on which to drive to the nearest town.

Who, they ask, needs the Internet more than ranch kids who are going to school at the kitchen table with a visit by a teacher from town one day a week?

The phone company answers all their letters and petitions courteously and, to some, hopefully. Better service is coming. Believe us, it's true. It was coming last year, two years ago and three years ago, and it is coming this year and next year and anyway some time before A.D. 2003, God willing and the creeks don't rise.

The letters speak of service and fairness and the company's anxiety to please, but in those letters, and in the letters received from the Canadian Radio-Television and Telecommunications Commission, one drearily discouraging truth emerges. Big Creek just isn't very important. Almost all of rural Canada is now no

140

longer important from a political or, to a large extent, from an economic point of view.

So if Big Creek doesn't like the phone company service, what can the people do?

Go to another phone company? What company wants Big Creek's business?

Boycott the phone company? Please don't make me laugh so hard; I may pull my stitches out. If the phone company knows a dollar from doughnut, getting rid of every customer in Big Creek would be a highly profitable exercise.

What pressure can people here apply? They're too few for their votes to matter and too poor to hire lobbyists.

Nor is it fair or reasonable to charge the big, bad company with being uncaring. That big bad company has shareholders, lots of them little old ladies who are widows of ranchers, and they expect the company to show profits.

Shall governments be blamed? Only if you can forget that government's duty is to do the greatest good for the greatest number, and the numbers aren't out there in the countryside any more.

What we might see happen in this country is the emergence of a new political party, similar to peasants' parties which survive in many European countries, movements devoted entirely to the forgotten few on the farms and in the forests. Such parties are never big enough to form governments, but they can be big enough to serve as spoilers in elections—people who must be bought off with concessions or, occasionally, a coalition government cabinet post.

Until that time, Big Creek keeps waiting for private telephones.

Line Up, Pay Up, Shut Up

BIG CREEK—When the rulers are planning a new atrocity to inflict on us, you often learn of it first in the rural areas. Perhaps their view is that if you plan some mischief, those people with straw sticking out of their ears are the best ones to start on. They won't organize protest parades or smear themselves with their own excrement and lie down on the porch of Government House.

This is, in fact, a mistaken view. City people are far meeker than country people. City people get news of new oppressions every morning with their corn flakes and coffee. They expect oppression. Almost always accept it. Only occasionally do they hold protest parades, and even then they have to call on American airheads to bus up north and bulk up the ranks of the marchers.

A recent atrocity has shown up here in Big Creek and will soon be common throughout this province, wherever landowners enjoy rights to use streams.

There's more than one moral to be found in this ominous story. It begins with Walt and Elsie Mychaluk, owners of the Bell Ranch. Each year, the government bills them for use of the irrigation water which they divert from Bambrick Creek. They always pay promptly.

Unknown to them, to the previous owners or anybody else here, the government has failed to bill them for one scrap of their land under a separate title.

This year the Water Rights bureaucrats announced that the Mychaluks were 17 years overdue in paying for their water. Kindly send $1,200, right now, to the Receiver General of British Columbia.

Elsie went to the office in Williams Lake and pointed out that she and her husband had owned the ranch for only 12 years. That buttered no parsnips, she was told. The owner of the property was responsible for all debts, old or new, known or unknown.

Why, she asked, had it taken them 17 years to get the billing straight. The gentleman explained that they were very busy in the Water Rights Branch and didn't have much time for keeping accounts. They sew not, neither do they reap, but my, they are such busy, busy people.

She persisted. Why, when their lawyer checked Land Registry twelve years ago at their time of purchase, did Registry report the ranch was free and clear of all encumbrances?

The answer will surprise many people who never heard of the Mychaluks or the Water Rights Branch. It will surprise just about anybody with common sense. Apparently Water Rights people do not speak or write or communicate in any way with the Land Registry people, they being in a different government department.

This is startling news to every farmer, rancher, placer mine operator or other citizen of B.C. who may be paying for water rights. Take note that when Land Registry declares a property free of all liens or other encumbrances, it does not mean it is free and clear. Some other bureaucrat may be waiting for you around the barn with a Norwegian slingshot.

Being one of those quietly persistent women, Mrs. Mychaluk asked if she could appeal. Of course, she was told. She was given an address in Victoria. She sent an appeal. It bounced back.

No way, said Victoria, go away. The Williams Lake office had made a mistake. (Again? Yes, again.) She was of a class of citizenry who are not permitted to appeal Water Rights bills.

We all know, or should know, that although all Canadians are equal before the law, some are more equal than others. Ranchers, it seems, are numbered among the less equal of the equals.

Well then, she said, the only thing she and her husband could do was refuse to pay.

Go ahead, said the man in the Water Rights office, but remember that when your vehicle licences come up for renewal, the Insurance Corporation of B.C. won't issue them to you because you owe the government money.

There's news for all of us. The state car insurance corporation is now also the rulers' collection agency, empowered to snatch money from us without all those tiresome court proceedings which private companies have to employ.

You can bet a thousand dollars to a pailful of horse turds that ICBC won't be refusing licences to dead-beat dads who don't pay child support as ordered by the courts. That's different. That money is owed to women and children, private citizens. Money owed to our rulers is a serious matter.

Overdue charges are piling up against the Mychaluks. When the rulers are 17 years late in billing, there's no penalty, but for the ruled the penalties start accruing 30 days after billing.

This is your government speaking:

"Line up, Pay up, Shut up."

You Want a Bridge?
Then Build a Bridge

ALEXIS CREEK—The Chilcotin, one of the larger and wilder rivers of this province, is now spanned a few miles east of here by a brand-new suspension bridge that was built so a six-year-old boy could get to school.

It is a spectacular sight, swooping down from a high cut bank on the river's northern shore, crossing 280 feet of rustling blue-green water, hanging at the southern shore on a 35-foot A-frame of peeled poles, and then plunging into the earth.

Spectacular it may be, but unspectacularly was it done. Nobody up here talks about it much. If you want a bridge, you build a bridge, don't you? Well, the Plummer family needed a bridge.

Wayne and Trina Plummer operate Neil Harvey's Deer Creek Ranch on the south side of the Chilcotin, halfway between the Chilco Ranch home place and the Duke Martin bridge near Alexis Creek.

They have two children, and as the oldest, Levi, neared his sixth birthday, they began to discuss how they would get him to the school bus on the Chilcotin Highway.

There is a road to the Deer Creek place and they could drive each morning and afternoon to the school bus stop—but this would be thirty-six miles a day and the road crosses an alkali flat that becomes an impassable bog many times each year. Sometimes they must keep vehicles on both sides of the bog hole, leaving one and walking across to pick up the other.

It seemed simpler to bridge the Chilcotin. That way it would only be necessary to build half a mile of road from the ranch house to the river bank and another eight-tenths of a mile through Dan Lee's ranch to the main highway.

Jack Casselman, a rancher noted for his handiness, had just sold his Brittany Lake Ranch and had some time to spare. The idea appealed to him. He had never built a suspension bridge before.

The other bridge builder was Wayne Plummer's brother-in-law, Lynn Bonner, of Riske Creek, who is the general manager of three ranches owned by Harvey in this area. He, too, was strongly attracted to the notion.

The bridge is called the Cassel-Lynn to honour these two entrepreneurs, but on the day I visited, Wayne Plummer was at the bridge, a hammer in his hand and a one-quarter-inch hand-rolled cigarette butt smouldering at his narrow lips.

"Jack Casselman did most of the work," he said. "He went down to Vancouver and looked at some bridges there. He said there didn't seem to be much of a trick to it. It took him about two-and-a-half months."

First, he pointed out, they bulldozed holes in the river bank and embedded concrete anchors, blocks twelve by eight by six feet.

They snaked one-inch cables across the river, slung them on the A frame on the southern shore, and Jack began hanging straps and laying planks. He just began at one side and ended at the other side, that's all.

(Wayne is not a talkative man. What conversation he had to spare that morning he spent mostly on the price of beef, which he summed up finally in the short philosophic comment, "What the hell, somebody's got to be poor.")

The details of the bridge, as elicited that morning, are that the main cables are one inch thick and capable of holding fifty tons, the drop cables are five-sixteenths steel and good for five or ten tons apiece, the crosspieces for the walkway are Douglas fir three-by-fours and the planking, one-inch pine boards.

It had, he agreed, cost Neil Harvey a lot of money. For materials and for Jack Casselman's time, he had spent $8,000. This, by a quick calculation, amounts to between one-twentieth and one-thirtieth of the cost if it had been a government project; but it wasn't. Even if the government had helped, the price would have shot up. Everybody knows that.

Trina takes the little boy across each morning and afternoon on the back of a motorcycle. When the wind blows hard down the Chilcotin valley, the bridge has both a ripple and a whip, she reported, and the fun goes out of cycling.

So they have obtained a brave old Volkswagen Beetle.

Wayne is now engaged in running vertical planks on the sides of the four-foot bridge deck as a safety measure.

The Volkswagen will still be too wide for the bridge but he calculates that he can haul out the welding torch, cut three inches off the fenders and running board of the car, and make a neat fit of it.

Trina and Levi will be grateful when the wind blows, the snows come, or when, as occasionally happens, the temperatures hit forty below.

Yes, they had a bit of a party when the bridge opened. Even broke a champagne bottle over it, after first removing the contents, which should not be wasted. But after all, it's just a bridge to get Levi to school, and was there any reason to write it up in the newspaper?

Stealthy, Healthy and Wise

BIG CREEK—To protect the innocent from their government, a few names and locations have been altered in this report. However, the shape of the problem will be familiar to all those benighted souls who live in rural British Columbia, and there may be a lesson for them in the problem's solution

The problem was an old, old bridge across a nameless creek on an unnamed public road. It's a trail more than a road, and only a couple of families use it with any regularity. The bridge had crude log underpinnings covered with planks cut with a chainsaw. The planks came loose and threatened to snatch the muffler off every car which crossed. The logs were rotting and sagging.

Clearly it was only a matter of time before a ranch truck broke the back of the old bridge and tossed its passengers into the little creek.

Although it's a public road and shows on maps as such, nobody in the country seriously expected the highways department to come in and fix the bridge. They've never sent a grader in there and nobody expects that either. Country people ask little from their rulers and are not surprised or upset when nothing is exactly what they get.

In this case a rancher, J. Smith, decided it was up to him to make a new bridge, at his own expense, and he went to Williams Lake to find out if there were any papers to be signed or permits to be taken out.

Indeed there were, in response to such an outrageous suggestion.

There were little trout in that stream and the rulers knew it. They were small, but so is the creek. Who could say but that those little sardines might some day make their way out to a piece of water large enough to make them grow to bite size. This, J. Smith was told, made it a federal matter and the federal rulers would have to drive out and look at the creek.

The ecology was going to be affected by tearing out those old rotten timbers, and who might say what the results would be. Clearly there was provincial government involvement, and also the Regional District, the body which makes up all those fascinating bylaws.

J. Smith could clearly see that getting permits to replace the rotting bridge would take months, perhaps years, in the hands of three levels of bureaucrats, all of whom are trained to the bureaucratic slogan: "When in doubt mumble, when in charge ponder, when in trouble delegate."

He told the government people he had changed his mind. He was not going to replace the bridge. It could stay.

Where, then, is the successful outcome of this encounter between the rulers and the citizen they rule?

The solution is there to see on that nameless creek on the nameless road, and would that you could be told where they are so you might drive there and admire the work.

Across the creek there is now a handsome little new bridge, thick, heavy new planking and steel reinforcing on the sides. The minnows still swim beneath it.

Yet everything is perfectly legal there. The old bridge has not been touched, not a splinter of rotten wood has been removed from it. It is there, intact. The new bridge leapfrogs across it without touching it.

Probably not one motorist in twenty who crosses that new bridge realizes that beneath his tires lies a heritage bridge, part of the treasured environment of British Columbia.

Of course the old bridge does continue to rot. Sooner or later it will fall into the creek, on the heads of those innocent little fish. If it's spring and the stream is in spate it may create an obstacle which will cause both it and the new bridge to be washed away. But that may take five or ten years, and eight years is the normal time to elapse between a government planning to do something and then doing it. So in the meantime there has been a good bridge to use on that old road.

There is hope for us all.

This Bridge of Hope, as it might well be named, is proof that with enough stealth and deceit, it is possible for the ordinary citizen to do good for his community in spite of three governments.

Incident at Duke Martin Bridge

The Downwind Tracker is wintering well in Chilcotin, but there are always interruptions in the even tenor of ranch life. One of his most recent is an episode that will be known in the folklore of that band as The Incident at Duke Martin Bridge.

One of the neighbours reports as follows:

"The Downwind Tracker left the ranch in God's hands the other day and drove off to Alexis Creek with his wife to buy some kerosene or drink some beer or argue with the forestry people or do something else that advances the beef industry in B.C.

"There was an ice jam on the Chilcotin River and some water had flooded the approaches, but he made it all right in his Volkswagen. The Downwind Tracker drives a Volkswagen now, and everybody agrees it is a good thing for him—this is one winter where the old, old problem of remembering to put his antifreeze in soon enough does not exist for him.

"In Alexis Creek he did whatever he had in mind for strengthening this province's economy, and they started back across the river toward the Chilco ranch about sunset, across the Duke Martin Bridge.

"It was about twelve below White Man's. (I guess you know that nobody in Chilcotin has accepted Celsius, but we are not so

151

much out of touch with the rest of the world that we don't know about it, so, to make things clear, we deal in Fahrenheit and call it White Man's Temperature.)

"His wife said she thought the water at the bridge approach looked deeper, but the Downwind Tracker said no, it wasn't any deeper; if anything, it was shallower. He has never found a cure for optimism.

"When he spurred the Volkswagen it lost traction pretty soon. That was because the wheels weren't touching the ground. It was floating.

"He has one of the old style Volkswagens which float. However, they also have a gas heater which vents to the outside and the river started running into the car through that hole.

"His wife pointed this out to him just about the time the motor stalled. When he opened the door the Chilcotin really began running into the car. She perched as high as she could on the seat and he got out and found himself up to his high pockets in ice water.

"He waded ashore, leaving her and the river there together in the car, and by luck somebody came by soon after in a truck.

"They got a cable on the Volkswagen and towed it back to shore. When he opened the door to collect his wife, the water all ran out and started down to rejoin the river. Her shoes floated out with the stream and they looked so funny that, although she had been a bit irritated with the old Tracker, she couldn't help laughing at the sight.

"Personally I think the Downwind Tracker is lucky to have married a woman with a sense of humour.

"They got the Volkswagen back to Alexis Creek where they got a room at the hotel. Next day, the car was dried out enough to start. Everything except the heater, that is.

"However the seats were all froze hard as planks and the doors wouldn't open. They had to go in and out through the windows, so they took it to the queer shop at Williams Lake.

"It took four days to dry out the Volkswagen and another day for the Downwind Tracker. I haven't found out what his errand was at Alexis Creek but I suppose it doesn't matter."

A Non-Romance
in the Moose Country

ANAHIM LAKE—This is the story of the big-game guide and the lawyer's wife. They did not marry. It is not a romance. Rather, it is a highly moral tale—one which will, I am sure, make better husbands and fathers of us all—females excepted, of course. The guide now speaks:

She was a customer that I will always remember. Always. She was a woman who made a very deep impression on me.

Her husband was a lawyer in the United States. She had left him down there and come up to hunt moose on her own. He was not with her. As I say, she left him down in the States. I guess that country could scarcely have operated with both of them away at the same time.

She talked lots about him, though. I felt just as if I knew him. His character was made very clear to me. Extremely clear. Absolutely clear. He knew all about how the United States ought to be run and she knew all about how my guiding business ought to be run. They must have made quite a pair.

We set out into the mountains with four pack horses. I was glad to have those pack horses along, quite apart from the way they so kindly helped us pack our gear into the hills. They were listeners, those pack horses, and she was a woman who needed a good listener at all times.

In the morning, she would start talking, a steady regular flow of words that never dried up until sundown. When she got out of her sleeping bag, it was just as if you had set the arm of a gramophone that never ran down. I felt that there was five of us to listen, myself and the four horses.

And I am proud to say that those horses all took up their share. There was not a slacker among them. For a fifth of the time I listened to her. Then I would look one of the pack horses in the eye. I would not say anything to that horse, I would just look at him. And he would know that it was his turn to listen. After a little time, he would kick the horse behind, or pass the message along in some other way, and that horse would take over the chore of listening to her explain how her husband the lawyer felt about the Supreme Court.

On the first day out, we did not have too much time to hunt moose or even to look at the scenery. From time to time I would point out to her the pretty colours on the poplars or the nice, clear, quiet looks of the mountains. But she would usually just say, "Yes, yes," and then continue to talk about whatever it was that I didn't want to understand. The second day, she developed a thirst about midday. I was not surprised.

"I must have some fresh water to drink," she said.

"There is some water there."

"No," she said, "that water is stagnant."

A mile or two later I found her some more water. No, she said, that water was not fit for human consumption. Every time I found water for her, it was unsatisfactory water. I never realized before that I had been poisoning myself in this country for forty-seven years. Finally, we came to a little creek.

"There is running water," she said. "That is the kind of water to drink." Personally, I had never drunk from that creek, because it flows out of an alkali flat. I started to explain this to her, but she got off her saddle horse, saying that this was good clear water and what a pity it was that I had been so long in finding it.

She remained very active all that night, stumbling over me in my bed roll as she wandered around the camp, talking about her indigestion. Next morning she said she had decided that it was the bacon that did it. I said yes, I figured it was the bacon.

We saw a number of cow moose, but cows were out of season then. She did not approve of that. She explained to me why a bull moose season was very bad game management. She went into a lot of detail on that subject. I have not retained all of what she told me. All I remember is the basic principle that you gun down every cow and calf you can find in order to build up a herd.

Anyway, to everything she said, I would always say, "You may well be right." Then if she pushed me, I would say, "Yes, indeed, you may well be right." This was usually all she required.

I think maybe that was the way her husband the lawyer talked to her also. He had neglected to enclose written instructions when he sent his woman to me, but that was all right. I hit on the formula independently. We had both struck it on our own, so to speak. Anything she said, I said, "You may well be right."

On the way out, we spotted a young bull moose. "I think that is a bull," I said.

But she knew all about moose. "That is a cow," she said. "It has no horns."

"You may well be right," I said, and we rode on. When we got back to camp she said that it had been a very unsatisfactory hunt. I agreed with her on that, too.

Spring Breakup

ALEXIS CREEK—All who love dirt roads and cheap whisky will want to note the most thrilling festival of the British Columbia interior which is called Spring Breakup. There is nothing in our cities to compare with it.

There are participants of the Spring Breakup jamboree kneeling beside the festival shrine—the bog hole—stuffing wood under spinning truck wheels, soaking their suits in mud, and calling loudly upon their Maker in tones of deep emotion.

Nature arranges few things for men more colourful, invigorating, and exciting than breakup.

Breakup takes a lot of preparation which Nature, in her methodical manner, does all through the long winters in the Cariboo, the Chilcotin, the Peace—anywhere that there are people to be inconvenienced.

Through winter's freezes and thaws, ice crystals form in the beds of roads. Sometimes they form a great lens of ice which remains invisible to the motorist as he speeds over it in those frozen months when the road surface may be as hard and smooth as pavement.

Then comes the thaw, and sometimes rain with it and, where once was road, there remains naught but a dismal tarn ripped by ruts two feet deep and filled with brown water rimmed with shell ice.

These bog holes appear in low sections of the road or where culverts have plugged. They also appear in high sections of the road where no culverts have plugged. Nature works in mysterious ways.

They have a custom of appearing, year after year, in the same section of road. This is handy for the highways people because they can tell, year after year, which sections of the road will cause complaint. They are thereby protected from unsettling surprises.

One bog hole of memory in Chilcotin was one mile long and ran straight and true between rows of black jack pine beside some little lakes named the Crazy Lakes.

The local residents were wont to petition for culverts and for gravelling. After a few years they petitioned for a bridge or, failing that, ferry boats.

The government eventually rebuilt this road and the locals have had to take their complaints elsewhere, but this was, in a way, a pity, for that bog hole was suited for a national shrine to the muffler and tailpipe industry.

I am no expert on bog holes, having never been stuck for longer than twelve consecutive hours in any one hole. Also my experience is intermittent. I haven't been bogged down since the day before yesterday at North Bend in the Fraser Canyon and it may not happen again for weeks. Some people get stuck every day at this time of year.

What can one do about bog holes?

Short of staying home, a cowardly course which our highways department recommends, one should pack a shovel, hip waders, chains, ropes and pulleys, an axe, a truck jack, food, tent, sleeping bag, and the Bible.

As you approach the bog hole stop and look at it.

Awful, isn't it?

There are chunks of wood floating in the puddles which

appear to be the wreckage of rafts on which some poor wretches have tried to make it to shore. They aren't rafts. Wayfarers before you have jacked up the back wheels, poked boughs and logs underneath, and, because they were lazy and laid the wood lengthwise, slipped off and bedded their car even deeper.

They should have laid the wood crossways for a corduroy road, as did their ancestors. Then twenty or thirty vehicles might have crossed this stretch before the corduroy sticks broke up, snatched off the muffler, and released the full-throated roar of the engine to the spring air.

Now having looked at the bog hole and thought these thoughts, you should put on the waders and walk into the thing, testing for bottom which is there somewhere. In the overlay you will frequently discover big sharp rocks which can punch a hole in your oil pan and a bit of blood where the careless folk have cut themselves on ice or tire chains.

In the most famous of Chilcotin bog holes the mud has a rare consistency, and natives call it the Fragrant Guano of the Great Northern Loon, Sweet Songstress of the Lonely Lakes, although they usually shorten the title.

By choosing your best rut, by rearranging any rocks, lunch pails, shovel heads, or other things you may find that won't float away, by chaining up the car before you get into trouble, you may make it to the other side where the road is merely sloppy and miserable.

Will you do that?

Of course not.

You will charge in. Halfway through the car will slow, give a gentle sigh, and come to rest high-centred and immoveable.

Now you know why you brought the Bible.

Silent Ken

BIG CREEK—When I suggested to Kenny Skomoroh that we take a couple of horses and try to pick up a moose, it was below freezing and wind was driving snow horizontal to the ground.

"Okay," he said.

I discussed the weather and the behaviour of moose at such times. Would they be in the timber or in the meadows? Would they be spooky? In short, were we likely to get a shot, all things considered?

"Maybe," he said.

We left the ranch at first light in a Merc one-ton truck that should have gone long ago to the Great Car Lot in The Sky. Half an hour later, we got stuck.

"Damn," said Kenny.

He worked us loose. We went on and stuck again.

"Hell," he said.

The third time we stuck he didn't offer any comment.

He spun the wheels. He shovelled. He spun some more. He unslung the chains, got out the jack, fixed the jack, jacked the jack, bruised his hands, haywired the chains, plied the pliers, and used a screw-driver for a chisel, with slush down his neck and mud on his face and the truck and two horses threatening to topple on him from the rickety jack and end it all.

Like other men of the country, he has the skill, the patience, and the endurance to take that old truck up a mountain and load it with glacier ice or fly it to the sky and snatch golden apples from the sun, once his mind be made up to it.

He got the chains on and raced the motor.

One chain came loose and whistled away over a meadow.

"Bastard," said Kenny.

He was up to two syllables.

He took off the chain and rocked the truck out, drove two more miles, backed the truck against a snowdrift to unload the horses off the tailgate and it stuck again.

I asked if this meant we would have to try chaining up again when we rode back here in the dark.

"Probably," he said.

Then I asked him which horse was mine.

"The brown," he said.

That shows, once again, that most people talk more than is necessary.

If I'd waited until he got aboard his pinto, it would have been made quite clear to me that I was riding the brown and there wouldn't have been all that talk.

After that I left conversation to Kenny.

Four hours later he talked some more. He stopped his horse, got off, tied it, and started building a fire.

"Dinner time," he said.

Later that day he pointed at a few poles on the edge of a meadow.

"Camped there once."

I pointed to a squared poplar post. "There's something written there," I said.

"Franklin," he said.

If I knew who or what Franklin was, he needn't say more. If I needed to know more, I could ask. The system works very well.

I did not ask.

Late in the afternoon I said I reckoned we had cut the tracks of three moose.

"I'd say four," he said.

We didn't keep that argument going any longer.

Sometimes we walked to get warm. On the horses we sat, feet frozen in the stirrups, hunched over, looking at the saddle horn as if there was an important message written on it.

He spoke five times to his horse. Three times he said, "Huhu, huhu." The other times he called it a knothead and a son of a bitch.

When the day was old and the sky was colouring, he stopped his pinto and held up one hand. Then pointed to a moose in the jack pines. Only bulls are legal.

"Cow," he said.

There wasn't anything more to say on that subject, so we rode back to the truck, fought mud, snow, chains, and sulky cayuses and got back to the ranch deep in the darkness. They asked what kind of a day we had had.

"Cold," said Kenny.

The rancher from whom I borrowed the horse wouldn't take payment but he said it would be fair enough to pay Ken a Class B Guide's rate for the day. I mailed Ken a cheque from Vancouver. It was almost the next summer before I ran into him again.

"You never cashed that cheque I sent you, Ken."

"Nope."

"You got it all right?"

"Yep."

'Ken, why didn't you cash the cheque?"

'Ain't needed it yet," said Ken.

A few years after this was written, Silent Ken and his girl-friend were shot to death in her father's log cabin by Crazy Joe, a recluse. Before dying, Ken got his rifle out and killed Joe. The couple's memory is preserved in two natural meadows of long grass nearby, Kenny's Meadow and Joanne's Meadow.

How to Die Chilcotin Style

RISKE CREEK—When John Rose, owner of Riske Creek General Store, was told that he had only three to six months to live he came back here and set about pricing coffins which, he says, are far too costly. The best price he's got on a memorial service so far is $1,500, but he is continuing to shop around.

John doesn't always exhibit this acute business sense. As readers may recall, when he let the Canada Post contract go to another store up the highway a few years ago he was delighted how much it cut down traffic in his store, giving him time to devote to important things, such as his gun collection.

He was always different and has entered into the legends of Chilcotin for some eccentricities, although reports that he sometimes shot at low-flying planes have been exaggerated.

"He isn't up yet today, but come upstairs and have coffee," says Sylvia, his wife. Sylvia is a tiny little doll of brown sugar and spice from Manila who never expected to spend 23 years at 40 below in Chilcotin, but love does strange things.

We drink coffee in the upper half of the big Quonset which is general store downstairs and home upstairs. There's a big box of morphine tablets on the table.

When John comes over from the bedroom there isn't much to do but mumble sorry about this, John, but he just says, "What's to be sorry about? Everybody's going to die."

"Yes, but if I were told I would be gone in three months, six at the most, I'd be resentful, I'd be saying 'Why me?'"

"I don't feel that at all. A lot of my friends in the air force didn't come home when I did. They died in their teens and their early twenties. Look at me. I was given another fifty years. Half a century extra. I should complain?"

Sylvia, who has always claimed that John is the original model of the Male Chauvinist Pig, brings over a card which he has written for use at his memorial service.

"Oh Lord, give our enemies the courage to apologize and to admit that we were right from the beginning."

This is partly aimed at the Goods and Services Tax people.

He says "A few weeks, a month or two from now, every GST man in Canada is going to come out and find all four tires on his car flat. That will be me. God will say, 'John, you promised not to behave this way,' and I will say, 'Not where those bastards are concerned I didn't.'"

Bev Ramstaad of the Gang Ranch, one of the old Cariboo Twan family, comes to visit and says, "John, I find this uncomfortable," and John tells her to get some sense of proportion into her head. "Think of me as the Titanic which has just been torpedoed," he says, with more sense of drama than of history.

Discussion turns to cremation and Sylvia suggests she scatter John's ashes on the flower beds she so wearily tends in this cold, high land. "No," he shouts. "Your damn dog will pee on me and I have never liked your dog."

For the record, John was born in Oldham, near Manchester, joined the Royal Air Force in 1941 and didn't get out until 1947, came to Canada soon after and was a technician in the Vancouver coroner's office for many years. "Maybe that's why death doesn't seem so strange; I must have handled thousands and thousands of bodies."

He married three times, gaining the title Revolving Rose, and will leave sons and daughters, the latest, by Sylvia, being still in the educational system.

The pain, he says, has been getting a bit worse lately, but there's always the morphine pills, and he trusts the doctors not to keep him alive artificially. "I could have spun it out for a year or two with chemotherapy, but what's the sense of delaying things?"

It's more than just being matter of fact. There is laughter in this room, warmth and the great mystery of human affections. John is showing how a gentleman cashes in his chips and quits the game.

The Old House
on Twinflowers

BIG CREEK—Beside a tiny creek called Twinflowers stands the old
Erickson house, square and sound as the day in 1904 when it was
finished. The pine logs were then yellow as dairy butter, but age
has turned them tan, then teak colour, then walnut and finally
almost black. Log houses in this country turn dark with age; log
fences turn grey. Nobody seems to know why. Do the families
who inhabit these buildings give off some aura which affects the
chemicals in pine sap?

This house had three sets of owners. First the two Erickson
brothers from Finland. They built it with broad axes and a whipsaw, beginning the work in 1902 and finishing it in 1904.

Neither married, although the picture of a lady who was to be
a mail order bride turned up under the wallpaper recently. Vic,
the younger brother, died in 1949, and in 1950 Charles sold to
young Bruce Watt of Chilliwack. Bruce came to Chilcotin to
watch the characters and became one himself.

The price was $18,000 for the house, the buildings, the fences
and a lot of land—but of course dollars were dollars then, not the
Monopoly money we use today.

There was inheritance tax in those days, and Charles so hated
the government that the sale contract specified that all Bruce's

time payments were to cease at his death so that nothing would be left for Victoria to tax. Because Charles didn't live long once he had no more work to do, Bruce got the place for $14,000.

Bruce and Phyllis Watt raised five children here. They dammed the creek to get running water in the house, papered the walls, added a small lean-to at the back and provided all five children with glorious memories of childhoods taken from a century before and uncommon, even fifty years ago, in Canada.

In 1974 they sold to the two Caddy brothers who, with their wives, lived there for a decade but made no changes to the old place which stood, solid as Anvil Mountain.

Ten years ago the Caddys sold to Tom and Colleen Hodgson, and they, perhaps with more affection for the past than the previous two owners, set about restoring the place to the way the Ericksons made it. They have added two graceful porches, front and back, and put in one large window, but all the rest of the considerable work they have done, including stripping away all wallpaper, has been to make it look as it did in 1904. They are awed by much they found.

The Ericksons' only tools were crosscut saw, axe, broad axe, augur, whipsaw and similar tools. There were no chainsaws to cut windows from walls, so every window of the four-bedroom house has pegged logs built from either side and not matching, one side to the other.

The floor, usually the first thing to go in old log buildings, is a floating floor, unattached to the walls. Today, after 94 years, it is level as a billiard table and free of rot except for a small section near the kitchen sink. The Hodgsons chink the space between floor and walls to keep out 40-below airs of winter.

Says Tom, "What you marvel at is the quality work that was done even where the eye never sees. There were never rooms in the upstairs, yet the logs holding up the roof were all precisely squared with axe work, just like the ones you see in outer and inner walls."

Life in the Erickson place is still special. The Hodgson children, Taunus and Michael, attend school in their living room.

There's no hydro, but there's a modern computer, only a party phone line but an entire wall stuffed with good books, sheep instead of Whitefaces on the place and a Toyota four-wheel drive as well as saddle horses.

One is tempted, direly tempted, to suggest that this should be declared a Heritage House. It is old, graceful, useful and represents one century of ranch life in British Columbia.

But the ghost of old Charlie would probably come raging back if he heard the government was taking some interest in the place, and probably Charlie would be right. The present owners cherish the place and look after it well. Once it became a responsibility of government, committees would be formed around it, studies would be commissioned, three more bureaucratic positions would be added to the civil service list, and sooner or later the old Erickson place would burn to the ground, after which there would be an official investigation, occupying three months and much tax money, so the guilty could be rewarded and the innocent punished.

Ruined by Clean Living

WILLIAMS LAKE—A few years ago Whitey Anderson leaned an elbow on the desk of Vancouver General Hospital information counter and said, "I understand you have an old, wore-out, broke-down, beat-up Cariboo cowboy...."

The receptionist cut him short. "Take the elevator to Three. Walk down the left-hand corridor. Bruce Watt is in 387."

Bruce was in the hospital, again, because he had trouble with his roping horse, again, while he was, again, trying to get the trick of becoming a world champion roper. He has pursued this goal for a long time, riding merrily down the road of life to the snap, crackle and pop of breaking bones.

He knows how to get the best out of horses, but horses know how to take the mickey out of him, and they stomp him, drag him and roll over on him.

When he owned the old Erickson place at Big Creek, Bruce was known to let precious good hay weather go by while he roped saw horses in his yard. Now, these many years later, living near Sheep Creek Bridge, he hasn't changed much.

Last January he was alone in the Williams Lake arena one night breaking a colt which bucked him off and broke his pelvis in two places and three ribs. Since nobody knew he was there that night, Bruce lay on the bark mulch for several thoughtful hours before somebody chanced by and got him to hospital.

He reports it was not as bad as another colt which went over backwards with him a few years ago. That one broke his leg in two places and also broke eight ribs, two of which punctured a lung.

On yet another occasion he got hung up in his rigging and a horse dragged him across an arena. "I didn't figure it was all that bad, but then I saw the fence coming up and the horse jumped it." The skin had been burned off his leg. They sprayed it with wax, but he had a near thing with gangrene.

He has had two plastic hip sockets built. He has had to take up steer roping instead of calf roping because he can't get in and out of the saddle fast enough to tie the calf.

Bruce is 67 years old now, and some people feel he is a little bit old for this sort of thing.

These people have missed a central truth about Bruce Watt, rancher, catskinner, logger, cattle seller, stampede official and joke teller. The towering truth—it is so tall people don't see it—is that this man failed to develop any of life's essential vices. He has never smoked. He has never touched a drop of alcohol. He doesn't gamble. He doesn't overeat and all his life has weighed what the insurance company tables say he should weigh.

There is his problem. He has none of the natural, healthy human failings which nature uses to jerk the rest of us around. Not for him the heart attacks, cirrhosis of the liver and the lung cancer which carries off normal people.

Fate it seemed, was helpless, left with no weapon with which to belt Bruce Watt behind the ear when he wasn't looking.

But the great primal force of the universe has a way of making everything fair in this world. She gave Bruce a passion for rodeo roping events, and as a result in the sunset years he is as beat-up, stove-in and broke-down as the regular sinners.

If there remains a question, it is this one: how did the Primal Bitch Goddess of The Universe keep up his interest in this horse foolery all his life?

It would be understandable if Bruce Watt's name was up in lights at the Las Vegas finals each year. But it never has been and it never will be. Bruce finishes in the money at Williams Lake Stampede and sometimes takes a first. That, and a few bucks won at jackpot rodeos, keep him in Miner's Liniment.

Roping is like so many obsessive-compulsive activities. There is hardly any room at the top. That goes for golfers, rock music stars, Metropolitan Opera tenors and dozens of other highly competitive activities. Many more are called than chosen.

If Bruce was destined to go to the top it would have happened to him by age 30 or, at the latest, 40, which was the year of Pierre Trudeau's first go-around as prime minister.

Thinking of such lamentable truths, I put the question to him: after so damn many years, why is he still roping?

He thought about it a while. Maybe the question had never occurred to the man before. Finally he said, "Because when the animal comes out and the rope barrier goes down, I feel forty years fall away from me."

Can you argue with that?